HIRED FOR THE Holidays

HEARTS FOR HIRE BOOK FIVE

RAQUEL RILEY

For Adam,
I'm so glad I listened to you when you asked me to tell your story. It's one of my favorites.

For Jones,
Adam and I both misunderstood you at first, but getting to know you was a pleasure I wouldn't trade for all the mistletoe in the world.

CHAPTER 1
JONES

As I swiped the mouse to awaken my computer screen, intent on checking my email, the intercom on my desk phone buzzed. Amanda, my secretary, informed me, "Mr. Marin, your two o'clock appointment canceled. I rescheduled them for this time next week. I also placed an order for your usual lunch delivery. It should be here within ten minutes."

I pressed the button to respond. "Thank you, Amanda. When the food arrives, just bring it in."

"Yes, sir."

For the next quarter-hour, I busied myself responding to emails pertaining to new client accounts. In particular, I was trying to strategize a portfolio for the Manson account. They didn't understand the first thing about hedge funds, market growth and trends, or cash management accounts. My secretary was working on a presentation to help ease them into the wide and diverse world of money management. I responded to their last email, making arrangements to entertain them at my condo on the beach over the holidays, where we could meet face to face to discuss my plans for investing their considerable wealth. Amanda knocked on my door before entering. She placed steaming containers of curried chicken and jasmine rice on my desk, its tantalizing aroma made my mouth water, and crossed the room to my mini fridge, retrieving a bottle of sparkling water.

"You have two more appointments today. I finished the PowerPoint presentation on the Becks and the Manson portfolios, like you asked. On your way home this afternoon, you have an appointment with the tailor at the shop you bought your suit from to have it altered. I'll send the directions and contact name to your calendar. All you have to do is sync your phone and it will update."

She ran polished fingernails through her short, highlighted blonde hair, tucking it behind her ear, before rearranging a stack of papers and sticky notes that cluttered my desk, creating a space for me to eat.

"Thank you, Amanda," I called as she slipped quietly out the door.

If not for her attention to detail and organization, I probably wouldn't remember to eat or shower. She scheduled everything for me, right down to my dates and my haircuts. I was usually so focused on business and meeting my clients' needs that I often let everything else slip by the wayside.

Damn. I leaned back in my chair and scrubbed my

face. The suit reminder made me aware of another matter I let slip away. I needed it for the Christmas party this week. As a partner in the second largest and most prestigious investment banking firm in the city, I was expected to attend every function my company sponsored. And there was never a shortage of them.

Family picnics with catered barbecue, bounce houses, clowns, pony rides, and dozens of children, not to mention hours of endless small talk. I felt exhausted remembering the summer picnic just months before. Every spring, we held a silent raffle and fundraising dinner, and every fall, a gala to raise money for the children's hospital. There were team celebrations for the youth athletic league we sponsored, and my least favorite, team building exercises like rock climbing, escape rooms, and volunteering at the local food bank.

I was supposed to find a date to accompany me to the party, another task that I failed to follow through with. It'd been years since I had a personal relationship. Becoming a partner at thirty-five meant sacrificing just about every form of pleasure in my life. I used to enjoy wine tasting, going to the theater, and fishing off the pier downtown. Now, if I was lucky, I might set aside an hour to stay in shape or sneak out to see the dentist during business hours.

Usually, I hired a date for these events. It was a cut and dry business arrangement and nothing more. I didn't have time to focus on my dates' needs at these functions anyway. I was too busy tending to my clients' needs instead. Keeping them satisfied was why we threw the Christmas parties and wasted thousands of dollars on them every year in the first place. After all, securing their needs secured my company's future. It was my only priority for the past five years, especially during the holidays.

Before I could forget again, I fired off a quick email to Amanda, asking her to arrange a suitable date to accompany me for the company's holiday circuit of schmoozing. I wished it were only one Christmas party I had to worry about. It was par for the course, but there would be no spending Christmas with my family or a long vacation in warmer weather. My holidays were always spent serving the company. I had clients to wine and dine, partners to meet with, parties to attend, and greens to golf on as I networked my way through the financial sea of sharks that swam around me, constantly circling for blood and my clients' accounts.

Between my afternoon appointments, I hit the gym on the third floor of my building—a rare respite from the monotony of financial paperwork. At four-thirty, I packed up my briefcase and bid Amanda goodbye on my way to the elevator.

"Mr. Marin," she called after me, "a moment, please."

I returned to her desk and set my briefcase down beside my feet, giving her my full attention. Amanda read the exhaustion on my face and smiled sympathetically.

"In regards to your earlier instructions, I was not able to secure you a date with the company you usually use. I believe we've waited too long and they're fully booked. However, I do have another company in mind."

The high-class escort service I often used ran a professional and above board business. They catered to businessmen and visiting dignitaries. I repeatedly gave them my business because they were discreet and the men they sent me had a certain look I was in need of. Clean-cut, handsome men, several years younger than me but not more than a decade. I didn't want to look like a sugar daddy. They wore the right clothes, said the right things, and pretended to be the polished sophisticates in my tax bracket that appeared to the outside eye as a suitable date.

I was openly gay in my business and personal life. Most of my clients and all of my partners had become accustomed to seeing the eye candy dangling from my arm at company parties. The escorts I hired had one job, distracting the wives so that I could talk business with their husbands.

"I'm sure whoever you have in mind will be fine. I trust your judgment," I told her.

After five years together, climbing the ranks by working late into the night, most weekends, and several holidays, I trusted Amanda with my life. If not for her, it wouldn't run nearly as smoothly.

"I was told by the woman who recommended them to me that this company employs a younger set of men. More college-aged." Amanda tapped her pen on the desk, a nervous habit I'd seen her do before.

Sighing with impatience, I picked up my briefcase.

The last thing I had time to do was sit here and debate the generational age gap between myself and my date. My time was better spent focused on more important things.

"I'm sure it will be fine, Amanda. Just give them the necessary information and update my calendar," I said before I hurried to catch the next elevator. I never liked to be late for an appointment.

I HADN'T FAST-TRACKED my way to becoming a partner by spending my evenings lazing around in my pajamas with my feet up, watching Netflix and snacking on a bowl of cereal.

It was nine o'clock at night and I was still dressed in my suit, sans tie and jacket. I sipped from a cut-crystal tumbler of bourbon as I read over Amanda's PowerPoint presentation on the Beck and Manson accounts. As always, she had done a fantastic job. The sound of my phone was an annoying distraction, diverting my attention from my notes. I set down my glass and my laptop before I reached for my phone. Not recognizing the number, I answered hesitantly. "Jones Marin speaking."

There was a beat of silence on the other end of the line before a man spoke. "Yes, hello. My name is Adam, and I'm calling from Lucky Match." His voice was smooth and deep, much like the bourbon in my glass. The seductive timber made my long-neglected cock twitch. "I believe I spoke with your secretary earlier? She set up a date for us and gave me your contact info. I'm calling because I don't think I can meet your needs, and I don't want to waste any more of your time."

Sudden irritation flooded me. The last thing I wanted to do was play matchmaker and spend the evening on the phone flirting with a boy. I had at least another hour of paperwork to look over before I could shower and get in bed.

"Why are you calling me? If my secretary made the appointment with you, then why not contact her directly?"

The man on the other end of the line inhaled deeply. When he spoke again, he sounded calm and controlled. Though I was irritated, I admired that brand of self-restraint.

"As I said, I didn't want to waste any more of your time, and I wasn't able to get a hold of her."

I gave him credit for keeping his patience with me. It could not have been easy in the face of my aggravation. "And why is it you feel that you can't meet my needs?"

"Because your secretary said that you were looking for a specific type of man. Usually, we have a number of escorts to choose from, however this week, they're all out of town for the holiday. I'm afraid I'm the only available escort on hand, and I don't fit the description you're looking for."

I appreciated his cultured grammar. While still casual, I didn't get the sense that he used words like um, dude, bro, or cursed excessively. He sounded like the kind of guy who said going to instead of gonna. That was one way to score points with me. Another was not to waste my time, but for some reason, I have no idea why, I was intrigued. No longer in a rush to hang up so quickly.

"Why not? Are you ugly? Missing your front teeth? Do you have a lisp or early onset male pattern baldness?"

The man made a choked, strangled sound before he answered. "No, sir. I have blond hair and blue eyes. Your secretary made it clear that you preferred someone with dark hair and dark eyes."

He was correct. Amanda would have specified that because it was a hard and fast rule of mine. My attraction to blue-eyed blonds ensured that when it came to choosing a professional date, I steered clear of them so as not to distract myself. But I had left it so late in the game that I was now out of options and couldn't afford to be picky. I didn't know what this man looked like, but he sounded and spoke like he would do just fine.

"What did you say your name was?" My voice was silky, cunning, as I satisfied my curiosity.

"Adam." His breath hitched. I found the tone and inflection of his voice incredibly hot.

I appreciated that Adam, while probably not giving me his real name, answered my questions precisely and didn't include a lot of unnecessary rambling. "Is there a way I can see what you look like, Adam?"

"My picture is on our company website along with my profile. If that doesn't satisfy your curiosity, I'm more than happy to send you a few pictures." *Would he indeed?*

I remained silent while using my laptop to pull up the website he mentioned, *Lucky Match*. After clicking the tab labeled personal profiles, I searched through a handful of young handsome men until I found Adam.

He was gorgeous, exactly my type. Adam Wells was everything I spent the last five years avoiding. His profile indicated he was six-one and two-hundred pounds. While two inches shorter than me, we weighed about the same. Which meant he was just the right size for me. The solid size of his body meant he was capable of challenging me in bed. His beautiful blue eyes were a deep shade of sapphire, and his blond hair was the color of honey with platinum highlights. Just imagining running my fingers through his silky strands made my gut tighten. I couldn't tell from the picture if they were natural or bought from the salon, not that it mattered.

He was younger than I expected, but the square cut of his jaw and chin gave him a more mature air. Heat stirred in my belly. How long has it been since I had a man like him beneath me? *Too long.* Adam wore his hair trimmed on the sides but left the top long enough to finger. It softened the hard angles of his rugged face. Would he flinch when I tugged the blond strands, or would he moan? Adam's full pink lips balanced well with his long, blade-thin nose, his beautiful jewel-toned eyes slanted slightly at the corners, like a cat. The man could be a model if he ever gave up on escorting. My cock twitched, begging for a chance to meet Adam.

He was beautiful—exactly the type of man I fantasized about when I jerked off in the shower. I had planned to only focus on business during this holiday, but with a man who looked like Adam, I might just pay extra for a spin in the sheets.

"You'll do just fine, Adam." I swallowed the desire in my voice, sounding calm and collected. An inelegant snort filled my ear. He probably thought I was an asshole, not that I cared about his opinion of me. "My secretary will send you a list of instructions tomorrow. Please follow them to the letter. If you have any questions, please contact her, not me. I will see you in three days. Good night, Mr. Wells."

"Good night, Mr. Marin."

The rest of my work could go to hell. After removing my clothes and hanging them in the hall closet for dry cleaning, I stepped into a steamy shower, palming my aching cock as I envisioned Adam's hungry lips milking me, until I shot with a satisfied cry all over the tiled wall.

Maybe this party wouldn't be such a tedious hardship.

CHAPTER 2
ADAM

What an asshole!

The audacity of that man speaking to me like that, telling me *I'll do* as if I was barely presentable. I'd bet five bucks all of that confidence and ego was wasted on a man who looked like Mr. Magoo—short, bald, old, and paunchy. Although if I were being honest, I really didn't care what he thought of me, not when I heard the offered amount from his secretary. It was about three times more than I was used to making for one date. If he wanted to pay through the nose, he could call me anything he liked. I would just grin and bear it, imagining my bank account growing fatter.

With Reid and Riley out of town on a ski trip with the rest of our friends, and Matt visiting his family for the holidays, I was the only escort available. In addition to handling all of the scheduling, I was taking all the clients for myself. My parents had chosen to go on a cruise this

Christmas, so going home wasn't an option, and as an only child, there weren't any siblings to visit either. It suited me just fine to enjoy the peace and quiet while banking plenty of extra money over the next few weeks.

Unfortunately, I didn't qualify for any scholarships, so the bulk of my tuition was paid for by my parents. I helped out where I could with books and registration fees, in addition to my living expenses. The small studio apartment I rented off campus didn't look like much, but it was clean and well cared for, and most importantly, it was mine. Anything was preferable to sharing a dorm room with a roommate and a bathroom with the entire hall.

The extra money I earned this Christmas would set me up to continue my education next year after I completed my bachelor's program. Someday, I planned to be the one doing the teaching at a university like Waltham. My major in English Lit put me on track to teach in the master's program, but I had yet to narrow down my field of study to a particular subject or author. I still had plenty of time to figure it all out. The problem was, I had too many favorites to choose from.

Bright and early, the following morning, Amanda Johnson contacted me. If Jones Marin was an abrasive asshole, his secretary was his polar opposite. She was warm and charming and instantly put me at ease with her bubbly laugh and gentle but reassuring tone. I figured she had to be a no-nonsense kind of woman if she worked for a man like Jones Marin, but you wouldn't know it by speaking with her.

As if he didn't already occupy the largest ego in the state of South Carolina, he doubled down by insisting that I appear at the specialty menswear store he frequented to be fitted for a suit. And following that, I was to visit a salon to get a haircut, a manicure, and a facial. Not only did he pay for the appointments, but he also paid for my time. Not that that made me feel any better about it. I'd been asked before to wear a certain something on a date, but the salon was a step too far. He had no right to demand I change the appearance of my body in any way. I was tempted to tell him to go fuck himself, but when I remembered the amount of money he was paying me for the date, I thought better of it.

Just grin and bear it, Adam. In three days, you'll never have to see Jones Marin again, and your books and incidentals next semester will be paid for.

At twelve-thirty, I walked into the menswear shop feeling slightly out of place. The slate floors and deep mahogany paneled walls made me feel as if I was standing in a Gentleman's Club instead of a suit shop. The man who approached me held out his hand to shake, introduced himself as Gianni and offered me a bottle of sparkling water.

Who in the hell drinks sparkling water while they shop?

My blood was set to boiling when Gianni informed me that Mr. Marin had already chosen my suit. *Of course he had.* Gianni explained that Mr. Marin had a particular style he liked best and chose the same suit for all of his 'special friends'. Like hell I was going to show up looking like every other rent boy he'd ever hired.

I browsed through the racks of formal wear, looking for something that suited *me*, not him. My pupils dilated when I saw the navy fitted suit. It would stand out spectacularly with my coloring. Gianni suggested a pale pink button up shirt, no tie. He said I would look more sophisticated by popping my top two buttons and using a pocket square. I tended to agree with him, after all, the man was a professional at men's couture. He added pale pink silk socks to the ensemble, and I even chose a new pair of shoes.

"Just add them to Mr. Marin's tab." Those seven words brought me immense satisfaction.

Gianni took my measurements, something I'd never had done before, and promised to have the suit ready the following day. He assured me that Amanda Johnson would have the suit delivered to me via courier so that I wouldn't have to trouble myself by returning to the store. After shaking Gianni's hand, I headed out to the salon.

If I thought the clothing store was out of my reach, it didn't hold a candle to the salon.

White marble floors, so glossy that I could see my reflection, held not one strand of cut hair. The walls were papered in a subdued silk print and dotted with crystal lighting sconces. A massive crystal chandelier centered the entire room. The little cubicle stations where the hairdressers stood to work were each walled in with frosted glass, giving each customer privacy until they looked their best. When I stepped up to the counter to check in, I noticed the shelves lining the wall behind the receptionist were filled with top-shelf products that I couldn't afford. I couldn't even afford to pay to have my nose hairs plucked in this salon, let alone the deluxe package Jones Marin had paid for.

Just who was this guy? With his expensive taste and demanding attitude, I was more than curious to meet him in person.

During my experience at the salon, I enjoyed myself more than I thought I would. I'd never had a manicure or facial before, but I thoroughly appreciated the pampering. I could get used to this level of self-care. My suit arrived, as promised, an hour after I returned home. According to the instructions Amanda sent, we would be attending a work thing at some fancy restaurant downtown. A quick Google search told me it was a five-star restaurant, the kind of place you needed to know which fork to use. God, I was so out of my element. Amanda offered to send a car to pick me up, but I felt uncomfortable letting them know where I lived since I never gave my address to clients before, no matter how much money they had. Instead, I arranged to be picked up at a coffee shop down the street from my studio apartment tomorrow night at six o'clock.

After my shower, I spent extra time inspecting my freshly exfoliated skin in the mirror. My pores had never looked so tiny! My skin positively glowed with health. Hands-down, this had to be the best haircut I'd ever sported. As I lay down in bed, I tried to picture how tomorrow night would go. I could only hope I didn't humiliate myself. These people had to be as swanky and superficial as Jones Marin. I imagined I'd be so far out of my depth that my toes wouldn't touch the bottom of the social pool.

Just before my eyes closed, my phone rang. It was the business ringtone that indicated a client was calling. "Lucky Match, how can we service you?"

A deep throaty chuckle resonated through the line. "Is that how you answer the phone to all your clients? So willing to be of service?"

I had a feeling I knew exactly who I was speaking with, but I asked anyway, just to be sure. "Who am I speaking with?"

"This is Jones Marin. Am I speaking with Adam Wells?"

So authoritative, like he was used to handling any situation, big or small. I didn't realize I was attracted to that kind of confident dominance.

"Yes, sir. How can I service you?"

He didn't sound as old as I pictured him yesterday when we spoke. Perhaps instead of Mr. Magoo, he was just a rich entitled asshole with *small dick syndrome*. SDS often caused middle-aged men with an inferiority complex and an overblown ego to act like dickbags, drive expensive cars, and demand things from people they had no right to ask for. I had a feeling Jones Marin had a bad case of SDS. Unfortunately for him and the others, there was no cure.

"I'm sure I'll think of something, Adam." The coy tone of his voice implied a double meaning. My heart rate doubled, thinking of all the ways he might make good on that innuendo. "In the meantime, my secretary informed me that you turned down my car service. She said you would rather meet at some hole in the wall café that sells coffee."

"That's correct, sir. I don't give out my address to clients. You can pick me up from the café instead."

Marin scoffed. "I could find out where you live in five minutes, Mr. Wells." His voice sounded so smooth, almost threatening. "Assuming that's your real name. I find it difficult to believe that a sex worker would use their real name." *The balls on this guy.* "I'm calling because I wanted to set the record straight. You don't make the rules here, I do. I didn't hire you to join me on some coffee date. I have business to attend to tomorrow night, and I don't have time for your games. I'll send the car service to pick you up at the coffee shop, or wherever the hell it is you feel safe at, and you'll meet me at the restaurant by seven o'clock, wearing the suit I picked out for you."

If I could reach through the phone and grab hold of his neck, I surely would have. The idea of squeezing until his face flushed and his eyes bulged felt immensely satisfying. His sex worker comment really chafed my ass. Technically, that's what I am, but the way he said it, injecting as much disdain into the words as possible, only made me hate him more.

"My real name is Adam Wells and I have nothing to

hide nor feel ashamed of. If you think so little of sex workers, why the hell would you hire one to dangle off your arm for the night? Wouldn't you want to project a cleaner image to your associates?"

After a beat of silence, Marin's velvety baritone caressed my ear. "Good night, Mr. Wells. I'm looking forward to meeting you tomorrow. Get some rest. With that ugly mouth, it sounds like you'll need your beauty sleep."

The jackass disconnected the call before I could reply. I was going to suggest he stuff his tie down his throat and choke on it. The sound of him gasping for breath would curl my toes. I loved that the first thing he would notice about me was the big "Fuck You" I would project by not wearing the suit he chose for me.

CHAPTER 3
JONES

That night I fell asleep rather quickly because, for the first time in a long time, I didn't have business on my mind when I laid down in bed. I couldn't get Adam Wells out of my head. Physically speaking, he was my wettest dream. He spoke like an educated man, and I could sense the fire beneath his words when I taunted him. I had no doubt that if I hadn't been paying him a small fortune, he would have told me to fuck off and cancel our date. Adam didn't think much of me, I could tell. Not that it made a difference either way. I was who I was, and he was here to serve a purpose. It was a simple transaction, and if it ended with sex, even better. But that was all it would ever be.

No matter how handsome he was, I was not looking for a romantic entanglement. And I would certainly never consider dating a sex worker. I could only imagine a scenario where someone I did business with would recognize Adam as their former paramour.

It was one thing to hire him for the evening to play a role. Many of my single associates did the same since we were expected to conduct ourselves as family men, even if we weren't. The idea of being attached lent us an air of credibility and wholesomeness. Most people that knew me would assume that he was temporary or hired. But if I acted as if we were truly in a committed relationship, and someone recognized him as an escort, I wasn't sure I could erase the smell of desperation that would taint me.

That Pretty Woman bullshit only happened in the movies. The people who ran in my circles didn't date or marry for love. It usually boiled down to money and connections. They married status. If they wanted to fuck someone that made them feel special, they did it quietly, behind their spouses' backs. They certainly didn't parade them at parties in front of everyone.

I trailed down my stomach, slipping under the waist-band of my briefs to palm my cock. Hard and hot, I stroked my length slowly, drawing out the pleasure as my mind tumbled through the fantasy of having Adam in my bed. The t-shirt he wore in his profile picture was tight. His body would be defined and beautiful underneath.

For a moment, I fantasized about teasing his nipples to hard peaks, sucking them into my mouth until he bucked underneath me. I would lick down his chest, tasting the trail that led south. Adam would squirm under the onslaught of pleasure as I tortured him slowly, sucking welts into his beautiful smooth skin. I gripped my cock tighter and pleasure burst behind my closed eyelids like white hot sparks. Quickening my strokes, I let my nails drag over the sensitive skin of my shaft as I imagined Adam thrusting his cock into my face, hoping I would suck it between my lips. In my mind, I took him deep into my throat, letting his juices coat my tongue. I bet he would taste as delicious as he looked.

He would plead with me to enter him, but I never gave in to other people's demands so easily. I squeezed my sac, relishing the sharp twinge of pain as I thought of how he would beg so shamelessly for my cock.

Just like the whore he is.

The pleasure in my balls built to an unbearable crescendo; my orgasm was close. I would take Adam slowly, making sure he felt like it wasn't enough as he fucked himself on my cock to get more. When he was sweating and mindless with need, I would finally give in and fuck him like an animal, pounding relentlessly into his body over and over until I shot deep inside of him.

I grunted my pleasure as I came into my fist. No, I did not cry out with Adam's name on my lips. I would keep that fantasy to myself where I could deny its existence.

A FRISSON of excitement hummed just underneath my skin all day as I anticipated laying eyes on Adam for the first time. Probably because I worked him up so much in my mind last night. I kept replaying his seductive voice as he greeted me on the phone, asking how he could service me. I was sure his company's tagline was designed to excite the men who called.

Mission accomplished.

This was why I steered clear of dating men who looked like Adam. It was too easy to obsess over the man considering how long I'd been single and alone.

At six-thirty, I received a notification from the driver letting me know he had picked up Adam and was on his way to the restaurant. I laughed at the absurdity of Adam thinking I would meet him at some common coffee house like this was a Grindr hookup. I didn't do dates. Tonight was strictly business, and if he wanted to earn another dime of my money, he would do well to remember that.

I waited inside the lobby near the hostess stand where I had a clear view of the valet stand just through the double doors.

Adam stretched his long legs out of the car before climbing out and straightening to his full impressive height. He was nearly as tall as me, another thing I liked about him. He waved to the driver, shut the door, and smoothed his jacket before walking inside. Fuck, he was even sexier in the flesh. The flutter in my chest ignited my anger.

That was not the suit I picked out for Adam to wear.

He looked amazing, like a California boy kissed by the sun and blessed by the gods. The dark navy blue of his suit contrasted boldly against his golden coloring. The cut of the suit was fitted, hiding none of his fantastic physique. The pale pink shirt he wore unbuttoned showed a hint of his toned chest and bronzed skin. My fingers itched to spread his shirt open wider and see what lay beneath. His pants pulled taut over his groin with each step he took closer to me, drawing my eyes to his bulge.

Adam was dressed to tease and entice.

Usually, I dressed my dates fashionable but bland, not wanting them to divert attention away from my conversations. He wasn't there to draw the eyes of the men and women I was conducting business with. He was only there to make polite conversation and babysit the wives. But with the way he looked, I was sure every eye would be trained on Adam tonight, including mine.

I made no effort to keep the irritation from my voice as I greeted him. "Adam Wells?"

His steps faltered as recognition dawned on him. "J-Jones Marin?"

I took great delight that my appearance rendered him speechless. It certainly made up for the fact that I jerked off to him last night. Any opportunity to even the score felt like a victory.

CHAPTER 4
ADAM

oly fuck! Jones Marin was freaking gorgeous. Like, *gorgeous*. His black hair, cut fashionably longer on top and gelled back, made his bright blue eyes stand out in stark relief. His cheekbones were chiseled by an artist, and his jaw was as strong and square as my own. I could tell from the finely tailored cut of his black suit that his body was fit and toned.

He had style. He had looks. He had charisma.

If only he wasn't such a dick.

I felt foolish for ever comparing him to Mr. Magoo. He was anything but. Jones Marin was not a middle-aged, punchy, prematurely balding man suffering from a midlife crisis. He obviously had his shit together, in all areas. It was clear from our previous conversations that he craved control. He had a dominant personality that probably served him well in business but wasn't going to get him very far with me.

I held my hand out in greeting, but he ignored it and pulled me into his arms, placing a soft kiss on my cheek. He inhaled through his nose. *Is he smelling me?* The thought sent a shiver up my spine as his fingers dug deep into my biceps. It seemed that my appearance would more than just *do* for him.

His breath ghosted over my ear, making my senses tingle. "You asked me how you could service me. I'll let you know soon." *Definitely a control freak.* He pulled back, loosening his grip on my arms. Pale blue eyes raked over my body, assessing my appearance. They glittered with an angry spark. "That is not the suit I chose for you."

Seeing his barely restrained anger boiling just beneath the surface of his cool demeanor thrilled me. "You're absolutely correct. This suit is much better than the one you chose. I thought maybe you just lacked good taste, so I took the liberty of choosing my own."

"Don't ever take liberties again. You will wear what I tell you to wear. That suit was selected for a reason." His jaw ticked as he ground his teeth.

"Look, Mr. Marin. I don't—" My words were cut short when he gripped my bicep again and led me toward the hostess.

"Come. I don't like to keep my associates waiting." He pasted a polite smile on his rugged face when he addressed the young woman. "Marin, party of six."

"Right away, Mr. Marin. The rest of your party is already seated. Please follow me and I'll show you to your table."

We followed her through the crowded restaurant to a

large, round table in the back with a beautiful view of the harbor. This was a dim lighting and white linen table-cloth kind of place. Our place settings were arranged precisely with all the extra forks I didn't know how to use and two glasses, one filled with ice water.

Two couples were already seated. Jones pulled out my chair and when I sat and scooted in closer to the table, his hand dropped heavily on my shoulder. "This is my date, Adam Wells." Jones took his seat and a sip of his water before introducing the others. "This is Susan and John Briggs. John is an executive account manager in my office." I nodded politely and introduced myself again, noticing that nobody mentioned what Susan did. Maybe she didn't do anything. Jones acknowledged the other couple seated to their right. "This is Marianne and Acton Sawyer. Acton is also a senior account manager in my division."

Again, no one mentioned Marianne. I nodded politely. "Pleased to meet you."

It dawned on me that I was the wife in this scenario and nobody cared to ask what I did for a living. They probably assumed this was all that I did—date rich men and pocket their money. People always underestimate a young man with a pretty face. Sadly, I had a feeling that with this crowd, a sugar baby wasn't an oddity.

For some strange reason, that made me sad. I felt an invisible weight settle on my mind, a weight made of melancholy. Was that all Jones expected or wanted out of his partner in life–a spoiled, selfish lover who viewed their relationship as a one-way street? And these ladies, didn't they care that they were being treated as empty-headed trophies? I didn't know them personally, but there had to be more under the surface than the facade I was presented with - pretty Barbie dolls who followed in their husbands' wakes, waiting for their weekly allowance to spend at the mall.

In that spirit, Jones ordered for me without ever asking if I had allergies or a favorite food. Begrudgingly, he nailed my order to a T. When the server placed our salads in front of us, I became nervous, my knee bouncing wildly under the table. As I studied the wives to see which fork they picked up, I noticed Jones' fingers tapping on my thigh. I assumed he was trying to settle me until I realized he kept repeating the same pattern. One light tap followed by a brief pause, and then another light tap. *One tap. One tap.*

He was telling me to use the first fork.

Jones drifted over my shoulder as he leaned in to whisper. "Always start on the outside and work your way in. It's the same with business as it is with table settings." I gave one brief nod to acknowledge his advice. "Make small talk with the wives without distracting us."

Seamlessly, he returned to his conversation with his partners but kept his hand on my leg. I waited a brief moment before acting on his suggestion, unable to ignore the heat from his palm.

"So, Marianne, do you volunteer anywhere, or are you busy enough at home?"

As I engaged Marianne and Susan in a discussion about their various commitments, which turned out to be more significant than I first judged, I felt Jones' fingers traverse my thigh before giving a solid squeeze. I glanced in his direction, but his eyes were on his partners. It was an oddly intimate gesture, especially since he didn't have to do it and no one could see it. Whatever his reason for doing so, I enjoyed the feeling. With every twitch of his fingers, every inch his hand gained on my leg, my heart kicked in my chest. How far up would he dare to go? Would he fondle me under the table? Would I let him?

During a lull in our conversation, I took a moment to study his profile. Not only was Jones a captivating man, he radiated power. His solid presence weighed at my side like a boulder. By nature, I was not a submissive man, but he somehow made me feel safe and protected just by being nearby. He fascinated me as much as he infuriated me. His personality was intoxicating.

I listened as he discussed portfolios and mergers and various things I didn't understand and had no interest in. It was impressive to see him commandeer the discussion. I had a feeling Jones Marin could twist anything to suit his purposes and still somehow make you feel as if you had the upper hand. He was a shark among guppies. A predator. With his dark coloring and quiet strength, he reminded me of a panther.

His fingers traveled closer to the inside of my thigh, and I had a fleeting thought that tonight, I would be his prey.

CHAPTER 5
JONES

His scent, his energy, everything about him invaded my senses and grabbed my attention. His bouncing knee drew my fingers in, the need to steady him overpowered my reason. It stirred my blood that he needed my strength, that he followed my orders and accepted my suggestions. It gave me immense pleasure to see such a strong independent man, so self-assured, act on my word.

I need him in my bed.

God, it had been so long since I had a man like him beneath me. My usual dates acted as if they were paid, because they were. We both went through the motions but there was no real challenge. It was a foregone conclusion that they would submit to me. Adam was stronger than that. He would challenge me. He would put up a fight before he gave in.

We went through the routine of saying goodbye to our company and as we passed through the doors I held open for him, I latched onto his forearm and tugged him to a stop. The frigid wind nipped at his hair, ruffling the blond strands like feathers on a bird. The colorful Christmas lights from the building reflected in his bright eyes, rainbow sparks danced in the blue depths. His smoky citrus cologne carried on the wind, filling my nose with his musky spice. We faced off against each other standing on the curb as we awaited the car service. Tension sparked in the silence between us.

"I thought you liked to take control." His throat bobbed as he swallowed.

I loved his show of bravado, that he found the courage to taunt me even when nervous. "Always." My eyes trained on his soft lips as his tongue licked over them, the reflected lights made them appear even redder.

"So just ask me then." His square chin lifted defiantly as he shifted his weight from foot to foot.

I imagined his throat and mouth were dry from his nerves. I'd love to wet them for him with my tongue. "Come home with me tonight." Adam hesitated even though he knew what I would ask. "Say yes."

"Yes," he breathed.

Oh, Adam, the things I'm going to do to you.

As we passed through the lobby of my building, Adam's gaze alighted on the lit Christmas tree decorated with beautiful hand-blown glass ornaments. I spared a brief thought for his holiday plans. Did he have a family he would celebrate with? Or was he alone like me, with nothing but work to keep him warm this Christmas?

When I pressed the button for the elevator, Adam's eyes widened when I pressed the penthouse button. "Nothing but the best, huh? Why am I not surprised?"

I schooled my features since I wouldn't give him the satisfaction he sought as the elevator doors closed with a soft hum.

There were two residences on my floor–one on either side of the building–both held spectacular views of the city skyline and the ocean. My condo itself was as ordinary as any suite I'd seen—black marble floors, white walls, and sleek but boring modern furniture. My decorator had gotten carried away with the leather and chrome aesthetic. I didn't spend enough time here to care one way or the other that it wasn't suited to my personal taste. I much preferred a warm and rustic decor. Nothing about my home described a single thing about my personality except that it was cold and barren, much like my personal life.

Adam's eyes devoured every minute detail. I wondered fleetingly what his impression was. Did it affirm his belief that I was an asshole? That I was a cold and ruthless and uncaring bastard? Probably. Adam flinched when I stepped up close behind him.

"Can I offer you a drink?"

He turned to face me. "Is that what you invited me up here for? To drink with you?"

Adam rubbed his hands down his thighs. His voice

sounded shaky, his wide eyes darted around the room before landing on mine.

"No, Adam, I'm not interested in drinking with you."

His pupils flared, eating up all of the beautiful color of his blue irises. "Then what are you interested in doing with me?"

What a loaded question.

"I'm interested in getting to know you better, but not through conversation and cocktails."

He backed up a few steps as I advanced on him. His wariness of me only heightened my lust for him. As I brushed by him, I shrugged out of my jacket, tossing it carelessly behind him to land haphazardly on the sofa. I continued toward my room, hoping he'd follow my lead. Unbuttoning my shirt, I turned to toss it on the chair and saw him standing hesitantly in the doorway. For a supposed professional, he sure seemed out of his element. Like he was waiting for me to take the lead. There was no position I was more comfortable in.

Adam advanced two small steps, taking in my naked torso. I noticed the distinct outline of his dick through his fitted pants, which were only growing tighter by the second. My body was tight and lean, and lightly dusted with dark hair between my toned pecs. I worked hard to keep in shape in spite of the many hours I spent seated behind my desk. At my age, it was easy to go soft when you were focused on work more than play. Adam's eyes traveled over my exposed skin, mapping my chest and stomach.

"Take off your shirt, Adam. Show me what I paid for tonight."

Squaring his broad shoulders, Adam lifted his chin and maintained eye contact as he removed his coat and unfastened his shirt, his long fingers working the buttons slowly, deliberately, in an effort to seduce me. He needn't bother, he already had my full attention. My mouth watered in anticipation of seeing what lay beneath. No matter what he looked like, Adam would be beautiful. Muscled or lean, hairy or smooth, pale or tanned, Adam's body was a work of art.

He parted the two halves of his shirt, exposing his sculpted chest and tight brown nipples. His skin gently rippled with muscle across his flat stomach. He was gorgeous, like a statue carved by the most talented hands. I closed the distance between us and reached for his shirt, sliding it from his shoulders and down his thick arms.

I kept my eyes trained on his as I reached between us to unfasten his pants, letting them drop to the floor as I smirked. "Get on the bed. Spread out and make yourself comfortable. I plan on keeping you there for a while."

His breath left him in a rush as Adam crawled onto the wide mattress without looking back at me. He rolled onto his back and made himself comfortable on my pillows. His tan skin glowed against the white duvet. He was the picture of health and youth and everything that I'd gone without for years. I intended to enjoy this night to the fullest, not sure when I might allow myself this rare opportunity for pleasure again. Not the kind of pleasure that I could find with any man in any bed, but *this*—pure carnal delight. *This* man, in *my* bed, was everything I'd dreamed of and everything I'd denied myself.

I had refused to let a pretty face and a tight ass sway my focus from making partner. Now that I had, I could let myself enjoy this one night with Adam. The only problem was that if I took too much from him, I might not want to give him back.

"Touch yourself, Adam. Show me your most sensitive places."

Adam held my gaze as his hands roamed over his chest and down his smooth stomach. He lightly rubbed his nipples, pinching and rolling them between his fingers until his hips bucked. *Definitely sensitive.* He dragged his blunt fingernails down his rippled stomach, tracing each dip between his muscled abs. Adam fingered his navel and he squirmed, his tan skin flushed dark pink as his breath hitched. The sound went straight to my dick. His left hand roamed over his hip bone, caressing the soft skin like a lover's hand. Then he smoothed it over his groin, cupping the cotton fabric covering his most sensitive place. He used his fingertips to tease over his sac, moaning when he made himself feel good.

I wanted to trail my fingers over his sac, to tug at the skin and trace the seam of his balls with my tongue. Once I put my mouth on him it would all be over, so I restrained myself by sitting in the chair across from the bed. Dark shadows cloaked my features as I watched him like a voyeur. Reaching into my pants, I wrapped my fingers around my cock, taking myself in hand and squeezing to stave off the rush of pleasure from the contact. I needed this to last... all night if I could.

"Slide your underwear off and spread your legs for me."

I watched as Adam complied with my request, sliding the black cotton down his thick thighs and kicking them off of his feet. He spread his thighs, palming the inside of one while his other hand traveled up his shaft. Adam was long and thick, his cut dick the standard they used to model dildos after. His hole peeked out between his plump cheeks, tight and pink, just like I imagined it would be. God, he was a fantasy come true, a wet dream. A poster boy laid up in my bed for my personal enjoyment.

"Stroke yourself for me, Adam. Show me how you like to be touched."

His long fingers toyed with his shaft as he trailed up and down the hard length with slow, tantalizing strokes. I felt every one of them ghost over my skin, spreading heat down my shaft.

Rising partway from the chair, I slid my pants and briefs down my legs, kicking out of them until they landed on the floor at my feet. I continued to stroke my shaft, drawing out a bead of precum that I smoothed over my swollen head to lubricate the glide of my hand.

What we were doing, touching ourselves in front of each other, seemed innocent enough. But in truth, it was straight out of one of my dirtiest fantasies. To have a gorgeous boy like Adam spread out before me, touching himself at my command. Bringing himself pleasure because I demanded it. In essence, my desire to dominate him was bringing him as much enjoyment as it was me.

And we had only just begun. I had plenty more games in mind for my doll.

CHAPTER 6
ADAM

W hat kind of sick and twisted game was he playing with me? I couldn't begin to guess what he had in mind. Usually, when a client paid to have sex with me, that was exactly what they did. They got on with it, got off, and called it a night, eager to reclaim their space and kick my ass out the door. Of course, Jones Marin had to be the exception to the rule. I didn't take him for a cheap man, but it seemed he was going to get every last cent out of my time and my body.

I was hoping to tease him and drive him out of his mind. If I could make him come while he stroked himself, I could get out of here before he tried to touch me. Although, a large part of me was dying to feel his hands on me. The other part of me, the more logical part, was trying to keep him at a distance. Some primal instinct of self-preservation told me that if Jones Marin fucked me, he would ruin me for all men. I didn't think it fair to let such a greedy and selfish dickhead take away any future pleasure to be found in other partners. After all, this was my line of work. If I couldn't enjoy myself any longer, then what was the point?

With that goal in mind, I ran the tip of my finger from my taint up to the tip of my shaft, tracing along the seam of my balls and the large, fat vein that ran up the length of my dick. I moved slowly, giving him time to imagine that it was his tongue. When I reached the crown, I dipped my finger into the slit and pulled out a string of sticky precum. Greedy for a taste, I licked my finger slowly and thoroughly, letting him see my tongue as it played around my finger.

I glanced over to see his strokes quicken, his cold blue eyes glued to my body, sparking with desire. His thick cock would stretch me deliciously, give me the burn I craved before the pleasure. He wanted me. I could see it on him, smell it in the air. He wasn't the only one with power. I aimed to make him lose control, something I guaranteed didn't happen often.

"Tell me how it tastes, Adam?" His voice, husky and deep, slithered over my skin like a caress. A baritone like that could make me hard without touch.

"It tastes too good for words. It's something you have to experience for yourself." By playing coy, I succeeded in making him groan. He sounded tortured.

Copying his movements, I stroked my shaft from root to tip slowly. I pegged him with my eyes so that he would have to admit defeat by looking away to watch me stroke myself. He finally did, and I assumed he loved what he saw as more fluid leaked from his tip.

"That's a good boy, Adam. Give me more. Move your hand lower." His fist passed over his wet head, catching and smearing his seed as he slid his hand lower. My tongue burned to taste him.

Jones wanted to watch as I toyed with my hole, fingered myself, but I would make him ask twice before I caved. I trailed back over my sac, squeezing lightly and tugging at my heavy balls, pulling them away from my body to reduce the amount of pleasure gathering at the base of my leaking cock. I traced along my inner thigh, tickling the sensitive skin. With one hand squeezing my nipple, I let my other hand roam closer to my taint. The skin there was warm and smooth and felt so good to touch. I pressed in slightly, and the pressure pushed against my prostate, making my balls ache. The tremor in my thighs gave me away. Jones was watching and he knew how much I was enjoying this.

"Lower, Adam. You know what I want."

If he kept that up my knees would be shaking like an unbalanced washing machine on the spin cycle. I reached further down, extending my fingers to the bottom of my crease and sliding them back up to my taint. On my second pass I pressed deeper, the tip of my finger disappearing between my cheeks. Raising my knees, I spread my thighs wider so Jones would have a better view of where I touched myself. I paused to suck my finger into my mouth, coating it with thick saliva before reaching back down between my legs. I trailed circles around my hole, teasing my voyeur. His breath caught on a gasp, the sharp sound ricocheting in the silence.

Closing my eyes, I gave myself up to the fantasy made real. How many times had I laid in my bed and touched myself like this, imagining a mysterious and sexy man watching me from the shadows, commandeering my pleasure? Too many to count.

I pressed my finger into my tight pucker and felt the ring of muscle give way as I pushed past the barrier. My gasp was louder than Jones's as I buried my finger inside of my heat up to the first knuckle. Slowly, I slipped back out before plunging in deeper. Goosebumps pebbled my thighs, making me shiver. The cool rush over my skin compared to the fire in my blood caused sweat to break out across my brow. I was quickly coming undone.

Though I had set out to bring Jones to his knees, it seemed I might surrender first.

"Open your eyes and watch me. See what you do to me."

The moonlight streaming through the window reflected over his wet shiny cock head, making it glisten in the dark. My eyes tracked every movement. I watched the veins in his forearm flex as he stroked his long hard cock. It was thick and straight, and I was dying for a taste. He looked so seductive, stroking himself like that. Now that I saw it, I couldn't look away.

"Tell me what that feels like, Adam. Don't keep me in suspense." His voice sounded rough, almost broken.

"Tight," I rasped. "So tight. And hot. It's smooth like

velvet and wet." He stood, still taking himself in hand as he approached the bed. Jones stood at the foot, looking down at me. His icy eyes burned with need. "I bet your fingers are thicker than mine. That would feel even better."

He bit his lip, showing me how much he loved that idea.

Jones's light eyes stayed glued to my hole as I fingered myself. "Do you like being stretched, Adam? You like to feel full?"

I moaned in answer as I added a second finger, curling my fingertips to brush my prostate. A preemptive spurt erupted from my tip, landing in the nest of blond hair at my base. God, I could tell my orgasm was going to wreck me when I shot. The heat built low in my belly, moving lower with each stroke of my cock.

As hot as this mutual show was, I half wished he'd just fuck me and put me out of my misery. But this exchange felt like a battle of wills, as did all of our interactions so far. Inviting him to fuck me would ultimately feel like giving up and allowing him to win. I refused to give in so easily the very first time he tested me.

Jones seemed like the kind of guy who was used to winning. Tonight, I was going to teach him a different lesson, and if he ever hoped to use my services again, he would learn.

"I like the burn, the first bite of pain before the pleasure. Tell me, Jones, do you like to feel full?"

Two could play this game. Let's see how well he did when the tables were turned.

Blue fire burned in his eyes, and they were narrowed on me. Jones stepped closer, his knees hitting the mattress's edge. "Is that what you like Adam? To feel in control?"

Fuck, he somehow had the upper hand again! He was a master of manipulation. I had no idea I'd find this so hot. I looked up again searching for his eyes, taking in his tall, dark, strong body standing over mine, drinking me in, and I was powerless to contain my orgasm any longer. My fingertips curled again over the sensitive bundle of nerves inside me, and I shot thick ropes of cum over my torso, the white liquid glowing against my tan skin.

Jones placed his knees on the mattress, looming over me, and with a curse, he shot over my stomach, adding to the wet mess. He braced his corded forearms on either side of my shoulders and leaned down.

"You're beautiful, Adam. But you look even better covered in my seed." And then he was gone.

The bathroom door clicked as he shut himself inside. A moment later, the shower turned on. Where just minutes before, I felt hot and hungry, desire coursing through my veins, I now felt cold and lonely. Isolated and disappointed. I never took Jones for a cuddler, but was a peck on my lips or the brush of his hand over my cheek asking too much?

It scared me that I never had that thought about a client before now. Minutes passed before he opened the door, and a rolling cloud of steam followed him out of the bathroom. Jones looked like a Greek god. His black hair looked even darker when wet. Fat drops of water glistened as they rolled down his olive skin, disappearing into the white towel wrapped around his hips.

"Though I hate to see you wash off my mark, you're welcome to use my shower."

A part of me wanted to refuse his offer, but a larger part of me refused to let him think I wanted to drive home feeling his cum drying on my skin. So I crawled from the bed and made my way to the bathroom. As I passed Jones, he gripped my shoulder, halting me.

"Even if you wash it off, you're going to smell like my body wash."

His dark chuckle followed me into the bathroom before I closed the door, shutting him out.

What an asshole! He was determined to come out on top, no matter what, and now I was getting hard again. Truth be told, I didn't mind so much taking his scent home with me.

CHAPTER 7
JONES

I gave Adam forty-five minutes from the time he left my front door to be dropped off at the café, make it back to his home, and to settle in before I called to check on him. My imagination conjured images of him lying in bed as he replayed our night. Maybe his hand was down his pants as he teased himself to the memory of my voice.

The cool sheets felt delicious against my naked skin as I lay in bed with the phone pressed to my ear, waiting for him to answer. I remembered the way his face twisted in sweet agony as he came. What I would've given to have him say my name when he shot his thick load. Adam was a worthy opponent—he knew what I wanted and refused to give it to me. His refusal only made me want to pursue him all the more, which heightened the thrill.

His smooth voice flowed into my ear after the third

ring. Shivers of desire rippled through my belly. "Did you not get your fill of me? Need a recap?"

So cheeky. I tried to recall the last time I ever considered that an attractive trait in someone but came up blank. But Adam wore his sassy confidence beautifully.

"I was just making sure you got home safely."

"Such a gentleman. Did you want to come and tuck me into bed as well?"

He was itching for my hand to redden his ass. I couldn't resist an opportunity to put him in his place. "I bet you were enjoying the smell of my soap on your skin so much that you didn't wash it off and now that you're lying in bed, your sheets also smell like me. Did you decide to forgo clothing so that the scent is more potent?"

I heard what sounded like a short puff of breath through his nose as he scoffed at my suggestion. "You are the world's most conceited ass. Did they teach you that in business school, or does it just come naturally?"

He couldn't see the satisfied smile stretching my lips. "You didn't deny that you're naked in bed, Adam. Were you touching yourself before I called? Maybe you still are? I'll be picturing it until I see you again the day after tomorrow."

That got his attention, as his voice became sharper. "What? On Saturday? I wasn't aware we had plans."

"Don't sound so excited to see me again," I teased. "My company's Christmas party is in two days. Naturally, I want you to accompany me. Tomorrow, Amanda will send you the details of your appointment with my tailor. And Adam? This time, wear what I chose for you."

"You could try asking me instead of telling. My mama always said you catch more flies with honey than vinegar."

"I don't ask, Adam, and I don't beg. I'm paying you well enough to agree to whatever I need. You can pretend that you don't enjoy it, but playing coy doesn't suit you. Sweet dreams." I disconnected the call before he could respond, knowing how much it frustrated him when I had the last word.

I chose something more stylish for Adam to wear this time. He would definitely steal the spotlight in the bold-hued fitted suit. So help me God if he wasn't wearing it when he showed up to the party on Saturday night because I was living on the idea of seeing him wearing what I picked out. Adam was going to be the sexiest man in the room, and it had nothing to do with the suit and everything to do with the fact that he followed my orders. For a man like me, who craved control, there was nothing more attractive than compliance and submission.

There were so many things about Adam that held my attention besides his pretty face and tempting body. I learned a lot from eavesdropping on his conversation with my partners' wives.

He sometimes surfed, which he'd been doing since high school. He studied classic English Literature at the university and was about to start his master's program where he planned on being a TA. He enjoyed reading and musical theater, and saved the playbills from every show which he displayed like art on the walls of his apartment. Adam liked Vietnamese food, and according to him, sucked at cooking despite taking a culinary class.

He had more facets to his personality than a diamond. The brilliance of his company made me want to polish each one until it shone. I imagined attending the theater with him, his enthusiasm elevating the experience for me. I could envision him in my rarely used kitchen, making stir fry in his underwear. That led to a whole host of fantasies I let myself entertain briefly before shaking them off and coming back to reality. Adam was an escort. He got paid by the hour, or the night, and I only had him for one week.

I'd spent the last five years denying myself the company of a man like him while working my ass off to make partner at my firm. Now that I could afford to loosen up a bit, I planned to take my pleasure while I could. I was going to make the most of my week with Adam and hope the memories we created were hot enough to keep me warm during the many lonely nights to come.

I COULD TELL Adam had a perverse sense of humor when he texted me yesterday with a picture of a powder blue leisure suit with bell bottom legs and a ruffled shirt. He had photoshopped his head onto the nightmare ensemble which he most likely found when he googled ugly suits from the seventies. I texted him back with a thumbs up emoji just to show I could take a joke. Though I wouldn't doubt that Adam could make that suit look hot.

He texted me again today telling me that the car I sent for him had a flat tire and not to expect us for another two hours. I knew that was a lie when I checked with the driver. He thought it odd that I asked him to send me pictures of all four tires. Adam was purposely pushing all of my control-freak buttons just to see me react. Not wanting to disappoint him, I planned on teaching him a lesson later this evening.

Even though I'd chosen his cranberry fitted suit, nothing could have prepared me for the sight of Adam walking through the glass doors of the country club. The man had swagger. He was sex on stick, as they say.

The jacket molded perfectly to his broad shoulders. The pants were tight enough that I could see the muscles in his powerful thighs flex with each step. I imagined his plump ass stretched the fabric nicely and couldn't wait to see the rear view at some point later. He wore a white button-down shirt that glowed against his tan skin.

Merry fucking Christmas to me, I thought as I licked my dry lips.

He was a present I wanted to unwrap slowly, all night long.

When he stood within arm's reach of me, I slid my arm around his waist and pulled him close to press a kiss against his smooth cheek. He smelled incredible, like smoky citrus.

"You look sharp. Not a speck of dirt on you from changing that tire."

He grinned slyly, revealing even white teeth. "I have many talents, Mr. Marin—using my hands is only one of them."

His taunt was designed to tease and he hit the mark. The innuendo coupled with the way he tested me earlier made my pants stretch tight in the crotch. My hands itched to put him in his place.

"We'll see about that later." I slid my fingers down his arm until I reached his hand where I seamlessly laced our fingers together. "Come. Let's get this over with. The sooner I conduct my business, the sooner we can begin to enjoy our night."

My sole objective for this party was to network and socialize, which would only take a tenth of my focus from Adam. Though, truthfully, nothing could steal my total attention from him when he looked this sexy. He was in his element, surrounded by the ladies and some men, shining brighter than the sun. He said all the right things to the right people, smiled when necessary, and laughed on cue—he was definitely a professional. Adam was polished and charming. He set out to be an asset to me tonight and he proved himself a success, as I imagined he was with everything he set his mind to. Five minutes spent in his company and you knew he was a likable guy.

But the real Adam, the one underneath the pretty smile and sparkling eyes, was the one I met two nights ago in my bedroom. The Adam that captured my gaze and dared me to be the first to look away as he stroked himself for me and whimpered from my commands. The Adam who came undone as I stood above him and spilled my seed over his beautiful body as he licked his lips, that was the man I wanted to get to know better.

My eyes scanned the room until I found him hovering over a plate of hors d'oeuvres, talking with my secretary. His head bobbed to the music as he laughed at something Amanda said and suddenly, I wanted nothing more than to dance with him. To take him into my arms, press him against my body, and sway together to the music. I wanted to feel his warm breath on my neck, the silk of his jacket beneath my fingers, his thighs pressed against mine. I wanted him to want me. Not just because I was paying him to be my date, but because he wanted me to want him too. I wanted to show Adam that I had more to offer than a head for business and a fat bank account.

Adam tracked my movement as I approached him, and my composure slipped away as he licked his lips, flared his nostrils, and quickened his breaths. I must look as hungry as I feel. When I reached his side, I bent my head close to his, letting my breath tickle his ear as I whispered, "Dance with me."

Without waiting for his response, I slid my hand into his and locked our fingers together, tugging him along with me to the dance floor.

We swayed to Christmas classics from the big band era as couples danced around us. I delighted in having Adam in my arms, twirling him, feeling his hips move under my hands. What was it about this man that drew me in like a moth to a flame? It was more than his good looks. There was something inside of him that beckoned me closer, to dive deeper and uncover his secrets.

"Are any of these people your friends, Jones?" His blue eyes were focused intently on my face.

"Of course not. I barely know most of these people. I just work with them. Why do you ask?"

"It gets lonely at the top, doesn't it? The guys I work with are some of the best people I know. Do you have friends outside of work?"

His questions made me squirm uncomfortably. What did it matter if I had friends or not? I didn't have time for friends anyways. What did friends even do together? Toss a frisbee? Grab a drink? How would that benefit my bank account or my career? I was sure Adam would say the point of friendship wasn't to have an impact on my career whatsoever. That it was time off work to unwind and have fun. My idea of fun wasn't found in a park or a bar.

"Would you like to be my friend, Adam?"

He tried valiantly to hide his smirk. "Do you even know the definition of a friend, Jones? It's someone who wants to spend time with you without wanting anything from you in return."

Did people like that even exist? Everybody wanted something. "So are you saying we can't be friends? Because I'm hoping there's something you want from me." I loved how his eyes sparked when I teased him.

Adam searched my face. "Maybe we can be friends with benefits."

"Do you have many of those?" The back-and-forth kept my dick at half-mast, threatening to break the zipper.

"No, Jones. Would you like to be my first?" he murmured, his voice soft and deep.

His question caused a cold shiver to race up my spine. We were both far from virgins, but the idea of being his first anything made me feel positively primal.

"Come on, let's wrap this up and get the hell out of here. I'd like to go cement our friendship."

CHAPTER 8
ADAM

The black stretch sedan that pulled up at the curb wasn't exactly a limo, but it was definitely a step above the car that I arrived in. Jones opened the door for me, and I slid inside, settling into the plush leather interior with a sigh. The extended legroom made it easy to move about and the partition afforded us some privacy from the driver. When Jones shut the door, the driver pulled away from the curb, smoothly merging into the busy holiday traffic.

Jones slid his perfectly manicured fingers over my thigh and squeezed. My heart rate doubled as he dug his fingers into my leg.

"Did you enjoy the party?"

"As much as one can. Something tells me I'll enjoy the after party much more."

I tried to sound coy but my heart beat so loudly I feared he might hear it. Where was all the air inside of this car? It was becoming difficult to take a deep breath.

Why was I so nervous in his presence? What made Jones so different from my other clients? The answer to that was *everything*. Jones Marin didn't have one common denominator with any man I've ever slept with. He was more intense, sexier, smarter, and more driven than any man I've ever met. The chemistry that sparked between us was hot enough to melt steel.

"Why wait? Let's get started now."

Jones flashed his wicked smile before sliding across the seat. He reached for the button of my pants as his lips brushed over the column of my throat. Scooting further down in my seat, I spread my legs to allow him more access. The idea that he might fuck me in this car made me incredibly hot, a warm flush stole over my skin. His hungry mouth sucked bruises on my neck as his slender fingers freed my cock.

Jones blazed a wet trail down my throat and chest, his talented fingers working the buttons of my shirt as he went. Parting the two halves of my shirt, he tongued my nipple and sucked it into his mouth before lavishing the other with the same attention. All the while, his strong grip stroked my cock, drawing moisture to the tip. I ached to feel his lips surround my swollen cock. His hungry mouth devoured my heated flesh as he lowered his head toward my lap, inch by slow, agonizing inch. I watched with rapt fascination as his mouth closed over my wet tip. Jones maintained eye contact as his lips slid down to the base of my cock.

He wanted me to watch him suck my dick. Although he was submitting to me, he was still in control. I breathed a ragged gulp of air, my tight chest heaving for breath as I fought to maintain control of my spiraling lust.

I palmed his dark head as he swallowed me, guiding his rhythm to show him what I liked best. His hot wet mouth gave me everything I asked for and more, sliding his soft tongue down the fat vein under my cock. Jones sucked on the sensitive engorged head as he popped off, then dragged his tongue through my wet slit, drawing out a sticky string of cum that he sucked between his lips. His eyes glittered with intense heat like blue fire, burning me up with his gaze.

The hottest blowjob of my life was about to be over faster than I could blink. There just wasn't any way I could hold out. I could already feel my tight sac drawing up towards my body, tingling with heat. My thighs ached from how tightly I clenched my muscles each time his tongue snaked down my shaft.

Jones slid back down my length as he palmed my sac, and when he reached the base of my dick, I shot down his throat. Heat washed over me in a dizzying wave, making me lightheaded with desire. He swallowed every drop and licked his lips as if savoring my flavor. Without pausing to think, I lowered my head to his and sucked the taste from his mouth. Jones chased my lips, crawling over my lap to get closer. He wrapped his hands around my throat, squeezing slightly as his velvet tongue brushed over mine. It was as if he was trying to swallow me whole as he tried to possess my mouth, my entire body, and the air that I breathed.

In this moment, he could have whatever he needed from me. I would give him everything.

Eventually, his passion cooled. Jones tucked me back into my pants before securing the buttons of my shirt. He brushed the wrinkles from my jacket and slid off of my lap, reclaiming his seat on the other side of the car. I immediately missed his warm presence, the reassuring weight of his large body in my lap. He watched me through hooded eyes, and I wondered if he had come while sucking me. Jones didn't seem like the kind of man to walk around with sticky pants.

"Thank you."

My voice sounded rough. It occurred to me this was the second time Jones had pleasured me without asking for the same in return. Was that another one of his kinks? I didn't think so, but I couldn't guess his motives. He had to be the only man alive who could be so selfless in his own pleasure, yet still make me feel like I was giving to him. Though I was the one who came, Jones made me feel as if he was the one who had come out on top.

The way this man twisted my thinking was a completely foreign feeling to me, and I felt out of my element. Lost in an unfamiliar world. He was spinning me in circles, and I was afraid I might not find my way back home when he finished with me.

Would that be so bad?

"We're heading back to my condo. Come upstairs and have a drink with me."

Jones rested his fingers on my thigh, and I hoped he

was searching for an echo of the connection we shared a moment ago.

The last thing I needed was more alcohol to further cloud my addled brain. I was one drink away from making some very bad decisions.

But Jones had no intention of serving me a drink. As soon as the door to his penthouse shut, he pushed me up against it and clawed my jacket from my shoulders. Breathless and dizzy, I clung to him as he ravished my mouth. His hands were everywhere—in my hair, untucking my shirt from my pants, at my zipper, and cupping my ass. His passion consumed me, laying waste to my inhibitions.

Screw the drink and the bad decisions I was about to make. All I wanted was for Jones to fuck me. I had no rational thought beyond that whim.

He walked me over to the couch, his possessive hands never leaving my body, and dropped into a crouch as he slid my pants down my quivering legs. Straightening up, he removed my shirt and turned me, bending me over the back of the couch.

"Spread your legs." His gruff command was more effective than any amount of foreplay.

He didn't have to ask me twice. I splayed my thighs as wide as I could and popped my ass out, praying he would fill it. Jones didn't disappoint. He dropped to his knees and dragged his tongue through my crease. The hot wet warmth of his mouth over my hole made me cry out for more. Jones sealed his lips around my pucker and sucked until the muscles began to loosen. His tongue licked into me, spreading me open, lubricating the way for his fingers.

"Fuck, Jones. Your tongue feels incredible."

I fingered my nipples, pinching hard as he licked me, and I was fully hard again and ready to go another round. My straining dick was likely leaving streaks of precum on the black leather as it was forced against the back of the couch with the weight of his enthusiasm behind me.

The hungry noises and grunts that slipped from his mouth as he feasted on my flesh made my dick drip. Jones slid one thick finger inside me and twisted as he slid in and out. He took his time working me open before sliding a second finger inside. The slight burn felt incredible.

"So tight and hot, Adam. You were made to take my fingers."

I pushed back against him, taking him deeper, and he cursed. Jones stood and stepped over to the side table as he rifled through a drawer. The rustle of the plastic wrapper told me he'd found a condom. A moment later, he was behind me again as the heat from his body warmed my back side. He positioned the blunt head of his cock against my hole, sliding it through my crease before pushing inside. When I cried out from the bite of pain, Jones groaned with pleasure.

"Let's see if you were made to take my cock as well. Brace yourself, Adam. I'm not going to be gentle with you."

As Jones tunneled into my body, his fingers dug into

my hips to anchor me against the force of his powerful thrusts. Gasping for breath, I imagined the bruises his fingers would leave and smiled. Each time he slammed into me, he scrambled my brain until the only thought I could latch onto was to beg for release. Bending lower, I arched my back, opening myself up to him fully. Jones bent over my back and licked a wet stripe up my spine before sinking his teeth into my shoulder. I howled in pain and pleasure as I felt my orgasm building with the force of a tornado. When it finally crested, I feared it would twist me up and obliterate everything in its path.

"Jones," I panted. "Sir, *please*. I need—"

Sir? What the fuck was this man doing to me?

Jones reached under me to grip my wet cock, stroking me with my own juices as he plowed me until I screamed, his name a plea on my dry lips as I came undone. He fucked me through my orgasm until my thighs shook and my legs felt limp. When he pulled out of my body, he straightened and stroked his dick with my cum, lubing his shaft before plunging back inside. Jones pummeled my used hole relentlessly until he buried his face between my sweaty shoulder blades and cried out, my skin absorbing the sound of his raw pleasure.

It felt incredible to hear him lose control, knowing I'd caused such a primal reaction in him.

He laid his head against my hot flesh as he fought to even out his ragged breaths. His cock softened and slid from my body, leaving me feeling empty. Jones straightened and placed a soft kiss to the base of my spine before disappearing into the bathroom. The sound of the door clicking shut in the distance reverberated through the silence. A moment later, the air conditioning kicked on, blowing a rush of cool air over my heated skin. A chill raced up my spine that had nothing to do with the cold air.

It felt like Jones had left a piece of himself inside of my body, tattooed into my flesh from the force of his thrusts. Without a doubt, it was the hottest sex of my life. Unfortunately, Jones would forget me the moment I walked out his door, but I wondered how long it would take me to forget about him.

CHAPTER 9
JONES

The hot water cascading over my back felt incredible on my tight muscles. Tomorrow, my body will feel deliciously sore. It had been a long time since I'd had such aggressive sex. My usual encounters with paid dates were more passive. I was lucky to even work up a sweat.

The way his body responded to mine so freely was addicting. His wanton responses showed me just how excited he got when I took charge. Adam was like a wild pony. He liked to sink his teeth in deep before he swallowed the carrot, or in this case, my cock. It was a heady mix of defiant acquiescence that made my dick hard just thinking about it.

Turning off the water, I stepped out of the glass-enclosed shower and dried off before donning my most comfortable pair of black pajama pants. My stomach rumbled, reminding me I'd skipped dinner. When I walked back into the living room, relief and delight swelled inside my heart to see Adam was still here. He'd redressed while I showered and was staring out the glass sliding doors that showcased the glittering city skyline.

"You're still here."

Adam turned sharply, his hand pressed to his heart like I'd startled him. "Fuck, you're unbelievable." He scoffed, shaking his head. "I was just leaving."

Damn, that came out wrong.

"I wasn't asking you to leave. Quite the opposite. I would like you to stay."

I didn't want to think about why he was in such a rush to leave. The sex we just shared didn't feel transactional in any way. It felt...personal.

"Stay?" Adam's face registered surprise. "What did you have in mind?"

Stepping into the open concept kitchen, I rounded the marble topped island and leaned on it, bracing my elbows. "Well, dinner to start with. Are you hungry?"

Adam stepped closer to the island, and I motioned for him to sit on one of the black leather stools. "Actually, I'm starving. I didn't eat much at the party."

"Come sit up here and keep me company while I make us something to eat." I fetched a pot from beneath the cabinet and set it in the sink.

His blond eyebrows arched. "You cook?"

I filled the pot with hot water. "When I have the time. You aren't the only one here with kitchen skills, Mr. Culinary Class."

Adam's mouth dropped open in shock. "How did you know—did you run a background check on me?"

Bitter disappointment pierced the joy I felt a moment ago. "Wow, I must have fallen very low in your estimation if you think that befits my character."

I was aware he didn't give me much credit for being a decent human, but a part of me wanted him to know the kind of man I was. But sometimes it was easier to keep people at arm's length than to let them inside. Would Adam even want to see inside my head and my heart? Would I let him if he tried?

In a fucking heartbeat.

His amused smile said he doubted that. "So you don't run background checks on people you do business with?" He looked expectant as he waited for me to confirm his suspicions.

The word *business* tasted ugly. Somehow, Adam had started to feel like more than that. "I pay attention to them. It's what I do best—gather details, acquire data and listen."

Adam's face soured. "Of course, I'm just one of your assets."

Placing the filled pot on the stove, I set it to boil and braced my hands on the counter before him. "Somehow we got off on the wrong foot, so I'm going to do my best to raise your opinion of me to a higher standard." Adam watched silently as I emptied a box of fettuccine noodles into the boiling water. "I have a condo on the beach."

He snorted in disgust. "Of course you do."

Ignoring his outburst, I continued to explain. "I use it to entertain clients, and sometimes, I drive over for the weekend and enjoy some downtime alone."

Adam pointed to the salt shaker on the counter, reminding me to salt the water. "I can't imagine you being able to unplug from your life. What if you miss something important?"

His sarcastic tone implied he didn't think my controlling nature would allow that. Following his instructions, I sprinkled salt in the boiling pasta and stirred it with a wooden spoon.

"Well to be fair, I unplug from everything but Amanda, who keeps me informed of all the important things I'm missing."

He eyed me curiously, watching every move I made. It felt like I was being judged by a Michelin chef. "That makes more sense."

The steam wafted into my face, causing my skin to flush. "I'm headed there this week. I'll be there for four days, and I would like you to join me."

His deep blue eyes narrowed. "Really? Just you and me? A romantic getaway on the beach?"

Nothing sounded better to me than that. "Is that what you would like, Adam? Time alone with me?"

Adam scoffed. "Hardly."

Moving to the refrigerator, I removed a package of prosciutto and returned to the counter. As I chopped it into cubes, I continued our conversation.

"I'll be entertaining clients that I invited from out of town."

"How did I miss that?" Adam replied sarcastically. "And you need me to fuck off with the wife at the beach while you discuss important things with the big boys?"

Forcefully, I laid my knife down on the cutting board and regarded Adam with a hint of derision. "Do you want to be one of the big boys, too, Adam?"

He slapped his hand down on the marble counter. The sound echoed sharply through the silent kitchen. "Stop playing your fucking mind games with me! I don't appreciate being patronized and manipulated."

I rounded the kitchen island and stood between Adam's legs, gripping his chin with a bit of pressure. "That's one thing I'll never do to you, Adam. I don't play games and I don't manipulate. What I do is figure out what I want and I go after it with a single minded determination until I acquire it." *And right now, what I want most is you.* Releasing my hold on his chin, I dropped my arm to my side but did not step back. "Yes, I have work to do, but it also might be nice to just get away for a while."

"So that's it then? Just business and a day off out of the office?" Was that disappointment I heard in his voice, or was it just my hopeful imagination?

My eyes searched his, hoping to see a hint of the answer I wanted to hear. "Let me ask you a question instead. Do you enjoy my company?"

Adam hesitated. "Our dates? Or our time alone afterward?"

"All of it."

He looked bashful as he admitted, "Yeah, I guess so."

Clasping Adam's hand in mine, I raised it to my chest. "I enjoy my time with you, and I enjoy your company. You're smarter than I gave you credit for, and it was wrong of me to underestimate you. When I'm with you, I find myself trying to steal an extra hour of your time. Inviting you with me to the beach sort of unites two halves of a whole. Business and pleasure." My lips pressed against his knuckles, dropping a soft kiss to the back of his hand. "Stop being so defensive and just allow yourself to accept my proposal. I promise to make it worth your while."

Adam smiled at me, a mischievous gleam in his eye. "When do we leave?"

CHAPTER 10
ADAM

For the thousandth time, I asked myself why in the hell I agreed to this?

The mirror taunted me with the reflection of my absurd outfit. Never in my life had I worn such a ridiculous sweater. Last night at the Christmas party, I made the unfortunate mistake of engaging Marianne and Susan in conversation, where they cornered me into attending a Christmas cookie exchange. Then, Amanda informed me ugly Christmas sweaters were the expected attire. *Fucking fabulous.*

I felt like an imposter. As an escort, and Jones's temporary date, I had no business attending a party with the executive wives. It reminded me of that game, '*Which one of these things does not belong?*'

But they insisted, and they were so polite, I didn't have the heart to turn them down. Having only been to one other cookie exchange in my life, when my mother invited the PTA ladies over, I believed Amanda when she told me this wasn't like any other cookie swap party I'd ever been to. After adjusting my sweater, which depicted two male reindeer *frolicking* indecently among pine trees, I headed out. How bad could it be? Just a bunch of ladies eating cookies and trading gossip, right?

Wrong.

My first clue that I was in over my head was when I arrived at the address I was given and realized the party wasn't being hosted in someone's living room. I parked along the street in front of one of the most premier bakeries in town. The large potted palms that flanked the bright blue door beckoned me inside. If this was a professionally catered event, they would have no need of my white chocolate dipped cranberry almond biscotti. Ignoring the fact that I spent several hours in the kitchen preparing them, I ditched the box on the front seat of my car, brushed the wrinkles from my pants, and entered the bakery.

Immediately, I was immersed in the smell of sugar and citrus. Glass counters showcased racks of gourmet pastries and beautifully decorated cakes. A long wooden table arranged with ten or so chairs sat in front of a wall of floor-to-ceiling windows that streamed in bright warm sunlight, despite the chilly weather. The table had been set beautifully with a white linen tablecloth, vases of fresh flowers, and large glass trays of cookies in every shape, size, and flavor.

Most of the ladies I'd already met were in attendance,

and they waved me over with smiling faces. "Adam, we're so glad you could make it."

I wished I could say the same. "Me, too! Thanks for inviting me."

Pasting a bright smile on my face, I took a seat next to Marianne and joined the conversation. Susan introduced me to each one of the smartly dressed ladies, though it seemed unnecessary. They all knew exactly who I was before I even opened my mouth.

The Executive Wives Club were all very interested in Jones's *flavor of the month*—my words, not theirs.

"So Adam, tell us, how are you spending your holiday?" Susan addressed me as she reached for a powdered sugar wedding cookie. Her pretty manicured fingers selected the perfect cookie and she nibbled it daintily, never dropping a crumb in her lap.

"I'm spending the holidays with Jones. Tomorrow, we're headed to his condo on the beach for the remainder of the week."

Despite their Botox injections, all of the ladies' expertly threaded eyebrows defied gravity, hitching up to their dyed and highlighted hairlines.

"You don't say?" Marianne looked positively titillated. This juicy bit of gossip was apparently more delicious than the cranberry macaroon she sampled. "Jones doesn't usually entertain his *friends* at the condo, only his clients."

Is that right? I can't imagine what would make me different from them. "We plan to be there for the next four days."

Kimberly, a woman I'd just met with long, flowing blonde curls added, "Jones has never had a long-term friend. We usually don't see them again after the second date."

Carol smiled behind her polished nails as she delicately chewed a chocolate dipped almond biscotti. "Could this be the one, ladies? We've never had a man amongst the ranks before." Her face soured as she turned the cookie over in her mouth before discreetly depositing it into her napkin. "This cookie leaves much to be desired. Skip this one, girls."

Their excitement gave me the uncanny feeling that they believed this was more than a paid arrangement. For some inexplicable reason, I felt the need to set the record straight.

"Jones hired me for the holidays to be his date at company functions. There really isn't much more to it than that."

Marion passed me a butter cookie dipped in red sugar. "Honey, a blind man could see the way he looked at you the night of the party." She turned her perfectly coiffed head toward Marianne. "Have you ever seen Jones dance with one of his dates before?"

"I can't say that I have." Marianne smiled mischievously.

Susan added, "And when was the last time you saw him leave the party early?"

Cecile answered her. "Jones Marin has never left a party, meeting, or business dinner early. He is notorious for being the last one to leave." She side-eyed me slyly.

"Until the dashing Adam Wells joined him." Cecile placed her hand over her heart as if the budding romance was too much to sustain a normal sinus rhythm.

"I think you've all gone quite mad. Is there alcohol in that?" I gestured toward the mug she held.

"Actually, there's quite a bit of alcohol in this. Let me order you one." She flagged down the server and ordered another round of toddies for the table.

Marianne finished hers off and discreetly wiped the sticky-sweet foam from her lips with a napkin. "Don't worry, ladies, my condo is close enough to his that I can see inside with my binoculars." She winked outrageously. "I'll keep you all abreast of the situation."

Shocked by her outright snooping, I scoffed. "Excuse me for a moment, I left something in my car."

I ducked out of the bakery to grab the box of cranberry biscotti from my front seat. It had to taste better than the one the bakery served, and suddenly, I wanted to share something with these ladies just as they shared their friendship with me.

When I re-entered the bakery, I placed the white pastry box on the table among the other cookies and flipped the lid open on the box, inviting everyone to taste my baking.

"Try this. I made them fresh this morning."

The wives looked intrigued, and each grabbed one from the box. "And he bakes as well? If Jones doesn't keep him, I certainly will!"

They devoured every last biscotti and asked me for

the recipe. The rest of the party was spent plotting and planning my wedding.

What fresh hell had I landed in? I was wrong to assume these ladies were harmless. Lesson learned—never underestimate the Executive Wives Club.

CHAPTER 11
JONES

Today was my last day in the office before leaving for the condo, and I had more loose ends to tie up than a yarn factory. Several accounts needed attention, I had two meetings scheduled, and I verified a portfolio prepared by a junior accountant was up to par. Amanda quietly shuffled into my office with a sheath of papers and files, ignoring my groan of misery.

"Good morning, Mr. Marin." Her chipper greeting, followed by the clack of her heels as she crossed the room, started a pulsing throb behind my eyes.

"Good Lord, Amanda, I haven't even enjoyed my first cup of coffee yet. Please don't tell me anything you're clutching in that iron fist of yours is a pressing matter." Setting aside my coffee mug, I reached for the stack she offered.

"Not at all. I just thought you'd like to know that your boy is the most popular member of the EWC."

Amanda's smile belied her casual words, and she threw the initials out like I should know what they stood for. "What boy? And what is the EWC? Are they auditing me?"

She chuckled at my frown as she arranged the papers on my desk. "The Executive Wives Club, and yes, they are definitely auditing you. Adam joined them yesterday at the annual Christmas cookie exchange party and passed his audit with flying colors. I'm not so sure you'll have the same success he did though." She tapped her lip thoughtfully. "He bought his vote with freshly baked biscotti."

I pinched the bridge of my nose, feeling frustrated and exhausted. I seemed to be missing a key piece of this conversation and Amanda enjoyed leaving me at odds as I scrambled to catch up.

"Please start from the beginning."

"At the Christmas party, the wives invited Adam to the cookie swap they held yesterday at a bakery in town. He accepted their invitation and showed up appropriately attired in an ugly Christmas sweater, bearing freshly baked biscotti, and won them over with his charming and friendly personality, much like he did to you. They have officially inducted him as a member of the Executive Wives Club, and the ladies loved his sweater so much, they bought you one to match."

It would take me more than an hour to unpack all of the information she just laid at my feet, but I decided to start with the easiest question.

"What kind of sweater did he wear?"

Amanda's smile turned positively devious. She lived for this. It wasn't often she found opportunities to have fun at her job. "It was a beautiful burgundy knit with white reindeer stitched in. The color will look wonderful on you when I line you up side-by-side to take pictures."

Pictures? With Adam? I was definitely missing many key pieces she left out of her story. "That doesn't sound too bad. How was it ugly?"

"Not so much ugly, as outrageous. They were gay reindeer, Jones, and they were having sex." Amanda delivered that with a straight face but her smile cracked through as she giggled.

"*Gay reindeer?* The reindeer were having... *relations?* And my partners' wives thought it appropriate to buy me one to match?"

It sounded like something Adam would choose. I wished I could have been a fly on the wall, observing him in his element as he charmed my partners' wives with ease. Never before had the ladies gifted me with anything more than a polite smile. Did they see Adam as the key to humanizing me? My icy heart definitely thawed in his presence. Probably from the volcanic heat he stirred up in my blood.

Amanda cleared her throat and continued. "It took me hours to track down, but I found one in your size. Adam will be stopping by at three o'clock to take a picture with you. He sounded quite happy to do it, and he's bringing you a biscotti."

Completely at odds with her usual stoic and professional demeanor, Amanda giggled about reindeer relations as she beat feet out of my office.

When she reached the safety of her office, she buzzed my intercom. "Just a quick reminder, you'll be spending Christmas Eve with Adam at the condo. You should really consider buying him a present."

The suggestion had merit. I could easily imagine the delight on Adam's face as he opened my present and then found creative ways to thank me for it. Whatever I chose would be worth every penny.

The more I learned of Adam and the more time I spent in his company, the easier it was to see a future together. He seemed to blend in with the wives like cream with coffee. I couldn't imagine a better way to relax after a long day at the office than to return home to Adam, cooking naked in my kitchen and sharing a glass of wine during dinner as we discussed our day.

In every scenario I envisioned, Adam was smiling, gorgeous, and happy to see me. Could he blend into my life as seamlessly as I fantasized? Would he even want to? Surely he felt the same chemistry between us as I did.

I thought about spending Christmas Eve with him. My clients would be long gone by then and I would have Adam all to myself.

What kind of gift says, 'Take a chance on me?'

CHAPTER 12
ADAM

The picture of me and Jones wearing matching sweaters was a definite keeper, though his grimace didn't match my grin. The hilarity of his misery made it priceless, and of course, made me love it all the more. Every time I unlocked my phone, the ridiculous picture cracked me up.

Jones was due to pick me up in an hour. There seemed little point in keeping my address a secret from him any longer. It's not as if he couldn't look me up—more than likely, he already had. With one phone call, he could learn my annual income, my parents' names, addresses, and their annual income, my blood type, my accumulated debt, and probably my favorite color.

I was more than a little nervous about joining him for the week at his condo. The jittery butterflies in my stomach had less to do with entertaining his clients and everything to do with sharing a bed with Jones. Not that we hadn't been naked together already, but sleeping beside him all night, legs tangled together as I snored in his face, felt way more intimate than sex.

It was coupley.

As I finished packing the final few items, my phone rang, the distinct beeping told me I'd received a video call. When I answered the phone, my friends' smiling faces crowded into the small screen. Their skin was pink from the frigid temperatures and windburn, but they looked happy.

"Wow, I got everybody at once. What's the special occasion?"

"Just checking to see if you bankrupted me yet." Lucky's red hair matched the color on his cheeks.

"Almost, but not quite. I guess you'll have to come home and save it yourself." My grin was playful.

"Not for another week. We're having too much fun." Lucky was shoved aside to make room for Griffin.

"Tell me you're not spending Christmas alone. It's not too late to fly you up here."

Here was a quaint ski resort in Vermont that resembled a Swiss chalet.

"Actually, I'm not spending it alone. I'm leaving any second to head to the beach." I hoped my cheeks didn't appear as red as theirs.

"The beach?" Reid's beautiful face joined Griffin's. "Who are you meeting at the beach? Christmas isn't for two more days. How long are you planning on being gone?"

Griffin looked more curious now that Reid made the situation sound more interesting.

"And with whom?" Cyan entered the screen behind them. His tongue poked his cheek in the universal sign of a blowjob. His beautiful cerulean eyes twinkled with laughter.

"No one. Just a client. Nothing to worry about. It's just business and I'll be home before you know it." I'm a terrible liar.

Griffin pointed at the screen. "When I get home, I want all the details. Be careful, and call if you need anything."

"And take pictures!" Reid added before Griffin ended the call.

There would be no hiding this *business trip*. It was unusual for me to make this much money this quickly. Lucky was going to want to know how it happened and Griffin wasn't likely to forget to ask for details. I only hoped I had something more exciting to share than mimosas with the wives.

With that thought in mind, I retrieved the board shorts from my bag and replaced them with a much shorter and tighter pair of swim trunks. There was no rule that said you couldn't lend fate a helping hand.

JONES WAS RIGHT ON TIME, punctual as always. I met him downstairs in front of my building. As his black sedan pulled alongside the curb, I waved. Jones opened the door and unfolded his tall frame from the backseat. He greeted me with a smile and a kiss on my cheek.

The heat of his hand burned through my shirt as it lingered on my shoulder. "I planned to retrieve you from your apartment. Is there a reason you don't want me to see upstairs?"

I brushed him off with a laugh. "I just thought we'd save time in case you were eager to get on the road. There's nothing up there worth seeing anyways."

Jones studied me for a moment, choosing his words. "I was very interested in seeing the play bills that line your walls."

Astonished yet curious, I asked, "How did you know play bills lined my walls?"

His rugged face shone with confidence. "Adam, I pay attention when it counts. And with you, everything counts."

Everything counts? After our last encounter, I felt Jones was trying to blur the lines of our arrangement. Now, I was sure of it. What was I getting myself into this week?

Shrugging carelessly, I played it off. "Maybe next time."

Jones reached for my black duffle bag. "Is this all you're bringing?"

Not comfortable with allowing him to accumulate favors, I hitched the strap more securely on my shoulder. "I travel light. No need for fancy suits like you."

Jones smiled like the Devil. "If you need to wear a fancy suit, you can wear me."

Where was this playful side of Jones coming from? It was unfamiliar to me, but I can't say I didn't like it. His bad jokes helped to put me at ease and smooth away some of the charged tension between us that kept my dick constantly hard and my heart pumping wildly.

After stowing my bag in the trunk, I settled inside the plush interior next to Jones.

"It shouldn't take us long to reach the beach. Traffic isn't usually too congested this time of day. In the meantime, why don't you tell me which plays you've seen and which you're still dying to see."

We spent thirty minutes discussing musical theater as we drove through the maze of traffic lights and bridges that brought us to the beachfront. Jones surprised me with his knowledge. He admitted to seeing quite a few plays and enjoyed the theater almost as much as I did.

When we reached his condo, his driver brought our bags upstairs where Jones tipped him before he left us alone together. And suddenly, the awkward tension returned, infiltrating the air between us with a heavy silence. As if Jones sensed what would calm my nerves, he started the tour in the kitchen, explaining to me the menu he planned to entertain his clients.

The Mansons weren't due to arrive for another hour and I hoped that was enough time to get my nerves under control. The kitchen was decorated much warmer than his penthouse. The dark maple cabinets and creamy granite countertops gleamed under the recessed lights that shone down on the large limestone tiles. A small island set with bar stools separated the kitchen from the dining area. Instantly, I fell in love with the massive dining table topped with the same creamy granite as the counters. I knew it was designed to impress his clients when he entertained them here, but hell, even I was impressed.

Off to the left was a large seating area set around a massive screen that dominated most of the wall. A large projector was mounted on the ceiling and the screen could be rolled up into a ceiling cutaway, hidden when not in use. Couches and chairs, dotted with silk throw pillows, were upholstered in a tufted light gray linen. Each pillow was a different bright hue to break up the monotonous gray. Coral and teal, sunshine yellow and fiery orange gave the space personality without being overwhelming.

"Would you like to see the bedroom?" Jones gestured toward the hall.

I swallowed the lump in my throat and nodded as I followed him down the hall. At one end was a closed door that I assumed was the guest room, and on the other end of the hallway was the open door that I followed him through into our bedroom. It was decorated in shades of light gray and navy blue, cool and soothing like the beach, but bold and masculine like Jones. I loved everything about this condo so far, including its location. I looked out the window over the tall driftwood-colored dresser to the glittering blue waters of the Atlantic Ocean that beckoned me outside.

Jones slid my bag from my shoulder and tucked it away in the closet. "Come on, we can unpack later. Let me make you a drink to help you relax before our guests arrive."

As he brushed by me, he stopped to rest his hands on my shoulders. Jones nestled up behind me and the heat of his body warmed my back. His breath tickled my neck.

"So tense, Adam. Perhaps later you'll let me help you unwind."

I wanted the moment to drag on and on as his strong fingers kneaded my tight shoulders, infusing the warmth from his hands into my trapezius muscles. Odd how I felt more comfortable with less distance between us. When Jones touched me or held me, my worries melted away and all I could focus on was his quiet strength.

Jones's reassuring presence felt right.

For someone who'd been independent for years, it felt strange to want him by my side.

The gin and tonic he served me was mixed perfectly, cool and sour as the first sip slid down my throat. We sat outside in the enclosed porch that overlooked the ocean. The cool breeze from the Atlantic danced across my face. My gaze followed the tiny sailboats that dotted the horizon.

It prompted me to ask, "Do you own a boat?"

Jones scoffed. "Spoken like a true sugar baby. I knew he was hiding in there somewhere."

I instantly regretted trying to make idle conversation. "I am the farthest thing from a sugar baby, sorry to disappoint you. If all you wanted was a man to suck your dick and spend your money, I can do that just fine."

Jones's eyes glittered dangerously, the dark blue

depths ignited with intense heat. "I don't want to be your sugar Daddy, Adam. I want to be your *everything*."

His honesty threw me off my game, and for a moment, I gaped like a fish, mouth wide open. "I'm sorry—that wasn't fair of me."

His eyes softened as the intensity bled out. "You don't need to apologize to me, Adam. I shouldn't have said that to you. I only meant to tease, but it came out wrong. I do have a boat and I would love to show it to you when our guests leave, although I suppose they'll want to see it as well."

I swallowed a large gulp from my tumbler and studied him over the rim as my throat burned with a sweet heat. "Our guests are leaving?"

"They'll only be here today and tomorrow. After that, we're on our own." Jones pretended to smile evilly but it came off as a sexy leer instead. "I'll have you all to myself. Whatever will I do with you?"

"I'm sure you'll think of something." Downing the contents of my glass, I stood and slid one of the doors open. I deposited my empty glass in the sink just as the doorbell rang.

Time to perform.

Yet, it didn't feel like a performance as I smiled and introduced myself as Jones's boyfriend.

I was grateful to have the entire day to process his words before being alone with him tonight in our room. What did it mean when he said he wanted *everything* from me?

CHAPTER 13
JONES

As I watched Adam answer the door, I tossed my head back and finished off my drink. *Fuck*. What if I played my hand too early? I'd only succeed in pushing him away. That was the opposite of what I wanted to accomplish.

But the more I thought about turning our arrangement into something real, the more ready I was to pull out all the stops. I only had less than a week to convince Adam to stay forever.

For the first time in a long time, I was focused on something more important than business. I wanted nothing more than to throw my guests out on their asses so I could have Adam all to myself. Landing their account didn't matter to me nearly as much as beginning the New Year with a commitment from Adam.

As it did with business, my gut told me Adam was a man worth investing my time and energy into. He was worthy of sharing my heart and my future. My instincts were never wrong. They certainly hadn't failed me yet.

I just needed to convince him I was a solid investment as well. That if he gave me his heart, I would multiply his love tenfold. That I was just as good a partner as I was a business partner.

"NEED A HAND?"

Adam looked so confident and sexy in the kitchen.

"Sure. Can you hand me the bottle of marsala wine?" He gestured to the brown bottle on the counter.

When I handed it to him, my fingers brushed his, sending sparks of heat through my arm. Touching Adam was like sticking my finger in a live electrical socket.

He shocked me every time.

I studied him as he chopped vegetables for the salad. The muscles in his forearm flexed with each swipe of the knife. The juxtaposition of his hard body with his gentle nature stirred me up inside. It was hard to remain still and not reach out and touch him. My hands itched to pull him into my arms and nestle my hard length between his cheeks. My lips longed to nuzzle his neck and suck tiny bites into his skin. Where Adam was concerned, I never seemed to get enough.

I loved to watch him work in my kitchen. My imagination wanted to pretend he was making a home for himself here, for us. But reality told me he was just doing the job I was paying him to do. Would Adam be here if I simply asked? There was really only one way to find out, but it meant risking my pride.

Adam thought my ego was overinflated, but in reality, it wasn't. I just happened to know the value of good things. My time and my heart were both precious commodities, but Adam, he was worth much more. In comparison, my pride was worthless. I could easily toss it aside for a chance of a future with him.

While our guests were occupied with drinks on the patio, I stole a moment to sneak up behind Adam, my hand over his as he chopped, my nose buried in his neck, breathing in his scent.

He allowed my touch without a hint of resistance—a good sign. I could feel the stress leave his body as he melted into me. It felt good to be what he needed.

In no time at all, this man had wormed his way under my skin and had become as necessary as the air that I breathe. His hobbies intrigued me. His looks mesmerized me. His personality entertained me. His heart warmed mine, and his body ignited mine. Adam complimented my life in every way. In two short weeks, he had rearranged my priorities and made me want things I'd been too distracted to notice I was missing.

My lips found the column of his throat, and I tasted his sweet skin.

"You must be hungry. Open up, let me feed you before you starve." He popped a chunk of bell pepper in my mouth.

I had an appetite for something other than food. The hard ridge of my cock pressed into his backside, and he ground his hips into me. Food was the last thing on my mind as I sucked the fleshy lobe of his ear between my lips.

"Behave. We have to get through dinner before we have dessert."

"Adam, this chicken is more delicious than the marsala I ordered at a five-star restaurant Scott took me to for our anniversary last year. You have real talent." Lillian Manson was full of compliments for Adam, from the color of his eyes to his culinary talents.

"She's right, it's absolutely delicious." Scott seconded his wife's opinion.

I studied Adam as he beamed from the well-deserved praise. His smile was more delicious than the chicken on my fork.

While Adam escorted Lillian around town earlier this afternoon, Scott and I had discussed business. I quickly realized that the money Scott was trying to invest actually belonged to Lillian, which meant most of our afternoon was wasted because I refused to discuss her money without her opinion.

After our meal, Adam busied himself in the kitchen, cleaning up the dinner while I discussed my plans with Lillian on how best to invest her money. To my great surprise, she constantly sought Adam's opinion. It seemed Adam had made quite an impression on her today and had won her over.

I admired the way he endeared himself to others with his natural grace and charm. I lacked his ability to connect with my clients on a deeper level. Adam was compassionate and empathetic. We were both good listeners, but Adam took it a step further. He felt with his huge heart whereas I'd remained detached and aloof. But together, Adam and I would make an unstoppable team.

I had two short days to show Adam how good we could be together.

THE DOCUMENT I was reading didn't capture my interest nearly as much as the symphony coming from my shower. I closed my laptop and reclined more comfortably on the pillows, just listening and enjoying the sound of Adam singing terribly off key. When the door opened, a rush of steam billowed out, followed by a very wet and pink Adam, half naked and dripping like a fantasy come to life. My dick instantly perked up as he bent over the bottom drawer to search for his pajamas.

He chose navy boxer briefs that hugged the curve of his fine ass. I prayed to God he didn't put pants on to cover his beautiful body from my sight. Adam slid under the covers, lying on his back with his head nestled into the pillowy down. My fingers trailed down his sinewy bicep.

"You were magnificent today. You completely outdid

yourself in the kitchen, and the way you meshed with Lillian and gained her trust so quickly impressed me. I knew you were amazing, but I was wrong, you're in a league of your own. You far surpass anyone I've ever met."

Adam turned on his side to face me, glowing from my praise. "I was just being myself. Lillian and I had a wonderful day together. I enjoyed her company."

"That's the thing with you, Adam. You don't even have to try to impress my coworkers and my clients. All you have to do is be yourself and they fall at your feet." Raising up to my elbow, I hovered over him, gazing intently into his beautiful blue eyes. "Just as I have. You've completely captivated me in such a short time." My lips descended to his, and our tongues danced and curled together. "You're stealing my heart right from my chest." My lips trailed down his throat, over his chest, seeking the place where he hid his heart from me. My tongue laved wet kisses over his heart.

"Jones," he cried out brokenly when my mouth seized his rose-red nipple, distended and tightly beaded.

I suckled the hard peak until he squirmed beneath me. His rigid length pushed against mine, and we both moaned with pleasure from the contact.

I moved further down his body, nipping his corded thighs and slim hips. My fingers tugged the band of his briefs down to expose his trimmed nest of blond hair. I buried my nose in his musky thatch.

"Mmmm."

The scent made my cock leak with greed. My hands

gripped the fabric, and I gently rolled them down his thighs and legs until he was completely bare for me.

I gently kneaded and stroked his aching balls. Adam babbled mindless praise as I gently sucked each tiny globe between my lips. His shaft flushed pink with arousal, and my mouth salivated to taste him. I sucked my finger into my mouth and wet it before easing it between Adam's cheeks to circle his smooth hole. An agonized whimper caught in his throat when my finger pushed against his tight pucker. He pushed back, begging me to enter him.

The glide of my slick finger through his tight ring set off a ripple of tiny shocks through his body. Adam breathed in fits and starts as my finger twisted in and out. His breath seized when I slid a second finger inside.

"So tight and hot. You're burning up for me."

Adam fucked against my fingers in wild abandon. His soft pleas were punctuated by little gasps that drove me wild. My fingers delved deeper into him with each rhythmic push.

"Please, please!"

"Only because you begged so nicely."

I sat up and moved to lean against the padded headboard and pulled Adam onto my lap. He was dazed momentarily as I positioned his legs around my waist. The heavy fog of lust cleared some and Adam circled his arms around my neck.

"Reach for the lube and slick my cock."

He obeyed quickly, grabbing the bottle and the condom laid out next to it. Adam ripped open the foil square and sat back on his feet to roll the latex over my shaft. Then he snapped the lid on the bottle and drizzled a dab into his palm. Adam stroked my cock from base to tip, coating my length in the slippery liquid. He raised himself up to line my cock against his hole and slowly eased himself down until he was fully impaled on my dick. His quick shallow gasps made it clear he was struggling to take my length. Showing no mercy, I entered him fully with one deep thrust and his agonized gasp echoed in the silence as the breath rushed in and out of his lungs. I was just as breathless as his muscles squeezed around my length.

He sat on the base of my cock, fully embedded as his muscles clenched around me, waiting for his breathing to return to normal.

"Hang onto my shoulders."

Adam dug his blunt nails into the skin of my back as he unclenched his muscles and opened for me. I pulled in a lungful of air and drove up into his body as my fingers sank into his hips. He cried out, throwing his head back, and I attacked his throat hungrily.

He felt tight and wet, and I wanted to stay buried in his heat forever. Spreading my thighs wide, I reached up to grip the top of the headboard.

"Fuck yourself on my cock, Adam. Show me how fast and deep you like it."

His eyes glittered with wild hunger as he gripped my neck tighter and rode my cock in a desperate frenzy to get himself off. I willed my orgasm to subside before I prematurely ended the hottest sex of my entire life. Adam reached for his dick.

"Don't you fucking dare. If you want to come, you'll have to do it without touching yourself. My cock is all you need."

His breathing grew more labored the harder he thrashed.

"I need your mouth, too."

Adam begged before he shoved his tongue between my lips and sucked my tongue into his mouth. I matched the thrust of my hips to the thrust of my tongue, fucking his mouth and his ass greedily. He whined into my mouth and changed his rhythm to grind back and forth instead of up and down. Each time he scooted back, his ass rubbed over my balls until they ached.

As his ragged breaths punctuated the air between us, I filled the space with desperate possessive words. "I need you, Adam... You belong with me... Your body and heart are mine... Come for me, show me my dick is all you need to finish."

"Fuck, Jones! You're all I need. You can have me, all of me."

With one final deep thrust, I shoved into him and buried myself in his heat as I came. My dick pulsed inside him as his walls rippled around me, milking every last drop of my pleasure. The friction of his dick trapped between our stomachs as he rode me pushed him over the edge. Adam cried out again as he came with a soul-shattering intensity between our bodies. I crushed him to my chest as the sweat cooled on our heated skin.

My lips nipped his throat. "I swear to God, I'm keeping you. Because I can't figure out how to let you go."

Adam rested his chin on my shoulder, his teeth sinking into the meaty flesh of my muscle. I welcomed his claim. I'd take actions over words for now.

CHAPTER 14
ADAM

When Jones said he had a boat, he hadn't lied. But he grossly underestimated the size of it. At forty-two feet, the double decker could technically be considered a small yacht. The bottom deck held two seating areas, one forward and one aft, and a single cabin with tinted windows for privacy. The cabin was small but luxurious, decorated in hues of pale blues and whites. A small galley kitchen fitted out in stainless steel sat adjacent to a narrow stairwell that led to the top deck. A bedroom sat beyond the kitchen. The room was mostly occupied by a plush king-sized bed and nightstands with a matching dresser in dark gray. An en-suite bathroom connected to the bedroom, kitted out with a glass shower enclosure and a slate gray vanity.

Everything screamed 'I have money', and I felt off-kilter as I climbed the stairs to the second deck. The entire level was a glassed-in sunroom with built-in pale gray sofas that curved along the walls. The three hundred and sixty degree view was absolutely stunning and an image of being fucked by Jones on the couch as we sailed the vast ocean, on full display through the windows, came to mind unbidden. I tamped down the thought before color rose to my cheeks and gave me away.

The heat from his body warmed my back before his hands even landed on my shoulders. He followed my gaze over my shoulder as we stared out over the glittering water.

"Are you still with me? Or have I lost you?"

I definitely felt lost. How could I connect with surroundings as rich and foreign as these? "My friend Reid would love this. He would probably say you were an exotic world traveler cruising to the south of France. Reid has quite an imagination."

"That sounds... extravagant." Jones chuckled softly in my ear.

"I bet you have never traveled anywhere in this boat besides a trip around the harbor. What is the point of all of this luxury if you don't even enjoy it?"

I could stand here all day and soak up his warm embrace and musky scent.

Jones rubbed his nose along my jaw. "Before you go thinking I'm a conceited ass again, let me explain. I share this boat with my partners. It's a company asset. And no, I've never used it for personal travel. Maybe I've never met anyone who inspired me to go anywhere. Perhaps things will be different now."

I turned in his arms and searched his handsome face for a sign that he might be teasing. "Seriously?"

He stared solemnly into my eyes. "I would take you anywhere you asked to go. Just say the word."

"Would you fuck me in this salon? In front of the windows on a sunny day?"

Jones's fingers dug deep into my biceps as he fought for control of his desire. It was absolutely fascinating to watch his feelings play across his rugged face.

"I would fuck you on every surface and deck of this boat." His nostrils flared and his chest heaved as he tried to calm his breathing.

I've never been desired with such depth of passion as Jones felt for me. Nor have I ever been admired for the things that made me unique. Jones saw me from all sides, and he wanted every part of me. It was a heady feeling. He didn't play games or keep me guessing. He always made his feelings and needs very clear, and I appreciated that.

Jones ran his hands down my arms to soothe me. "Are you hungry? I can feed you before we have fun."

"I'm too nervous to eat. What kind of fun did you have planned?"

My stomach roiled in knots from his honest and unexpected bold declarations. I didn't know how to feel. Part of me wanted to buy everything he was selling me. But what if that was all it was? A sales pitch?

Then again, he'd already paid for my time and my body, so there wasn't much left to sell me on. Maybe he really was sincere?

Jones grinned. "Snorkeling, followed by dinner on deck."

My eyes widened. "Snorkeling? You want me to get in the water?"

"Don't worry, I'll protect you from the big scary fish with sharp teeth."

This time when Jones grinned, he looked like the predators he promised to protect me from.

"Maybe I should be more scared of you?"

"Maybe you should." Jones cupped my cheek, his thumb caressed my jaw. "Adam, I hope you spend many more days and nights on this yacht in the future, but for the sake of pretending for my clients, can you act as if this isn't your first time aboard?"

My smile was easy and playful. "Sure. I'll try to look less impressed."

WE DONNED wetsuits and gathered on deck. Scott opted to join us, but Lillian chose to stay on deck and sunbathe. My eyes lingered on Jones's powerful frame. His wetsuit clung tightly to every curve and bulge, and my hands itched to touch him. When he noticed my hungry stare, he smirked knowingly.

The icy water chilled me through the thick layers of neoprene and numbed my exposed face. I showed Scott how to acclimate his mask with salt water to reduce fogging and helped fix his snorkel in place before diving below the surface. Jones had moored us close to a man-made reef created by sinking an old boat. The reef teemed with life. Scott followed behind me as I pointed out colorful coral and bright neon fish in every color of the rainbow.

I felt a slight tug on my leg and looked back to see that Jones had caught up with me. He crawled up the length of my body and removed the mouthpiece of my snorkel. Jones sealed his lips over mine and breathed into my lungs. His tongue snaked out to tangle with mine as we shared the same breath. Then, he replaced my mouthpiece and pushed himself up to break through the surface of the water for a real breath, leaving me hard and wanting in my wetsuit.

When I surfaced and climbed aboard, Jones was waiting with a towel warmed from the sun. As he unzipped my wetsuit, his hungry eyes devoured every inch of my skin as he exposed it to the frigid wind. My nipples tightened painfully and I rubbed them with the towel to loosen the overly sensitive nubs. Jones licked his lips as he stared, and I wanted nothing more than to toss the Mansons overboard and drag Jones into a warm steamy shower with me. His possessive gaze would have to be enough to keep me warm instead.

Later that night, the stars glittered like diamonds in the inky velvet sky. The wind died down to a chilly breeze and felt refreshing as we sat on deck and ate a delicious seafood pasta and crisp salad. The white wine fizzed delightfully on my tongue, cutting through the heavy cream sauce on the pasta and refreshing my palate. It was a perfect evening with good company, excellent food, and Jones's warm hand on my thigh under the table.

After we cleared away the remnants of our meal, Jones cruised back to the marina where we disembarked and drove the short distance back to the condo. As soon as we walked inside, the Mansons retired to their room and Jones and I headed to ours. I fell asleep before my head even hit the pillow.

CHAPTER 15
JONES

He's so beautiful.

Adam might possibly have the longest lashes I'd ever seen on a man. His pillowy soft lips looked extra plump from the way his cheek squished against the pillow. I was dying to kiss them again, but I dared not wake him. He looked exhausted from the sun and the swimming, and he needed his rest. Besides, I had other plans for him tonight.

After placing a phone call to the concierge, and another to Amanda, I showered and went about setting my plan in motion. Everything I'd come to hope for over the last two weeks was riding on tomorrow morning. In a few short hours, I would know whether Adam accepted or rejected my proposal. His answer would tell me everything I needed to know about whether he returned my affection or was merely doing a job he was being paid handsomely for.

My stomach roiled with nervous energy. I popped the

top off a cut-crystal decanter and poured two fingers of bourbon into a squat glass. The bourbon tasted buttery and warm as it blazed a trail of heat down my throat, settling my nerves. I'd never before allowed myself to take such an uncalculated risk, in business or my personal life. The feeling was unfamiliar and unwelcomed, but would be more than worthwhile if it turned out in my favor.

And if it didn't? No, Adam felt something for me, I was sure of it. The man had many talents but acting wasn't one of them. His sincerity was one of the things I loved most about him.

I spent the next several hours making sure everything was just right before finally settling into bed beside Adam. His warm body beckoned me, and I felt a twinge of disappointment that I hadn't made love to him today. But if things worked out in the morning, there would be plenty of opportunities for that in the future.

Patience was a virtue, and I could wait for Adam virtuously.

I pulled him against my chest and nestled up to his back, tangling our legs together as I reached my arm across his stomach. Even unconscious, Adam nestled into my warmth with a kitten-like purr of satisfaction. With my nose buried into his neck, I breathed in his scent as I drifted off to sleep.

$\approx$

THE WET WARMTH of Adam's tongue blazed a fiery trail of desire down my stomach. My eyes fluttered open as a deep groan rolled out of my throat. My hand cupped the back of his blond head, urging him lower. He fingered the waistband of my briefs and tugged them below my balls. Adam's hot mouth slipped down my shaft and back up again, wetting the length. His full lips stretched over the fat crown, and he sucked me into his mouth, taking most of my length in one swallow.

"God, yes. Suck me, Adam." If this was what it was like to wake up with him, sign me up for a lifetime.

His wicked tongue worked its magic until I felt the muscles tighten below the base of my cock. Heat flooded my groin as my orgasm rushed over me, and I came in thick waves down his throat. Adam hummed as he swallowed. The vibration tickled my swollen, sensitized flesh. He smiled and licked his lips, as if grateful for every drop I gifted him. My thumb traced over his glistening lips and wiped away the sticky remnants of my seed.

"Your fucking mouth is—" Adam cut my words short as he attacked my mouth with hungry urgency. He stroked my tongue, and I tasted my bittersweet flavor in his kiss. "Damn. Are you always this eager in the morning?"

He rolled to his side, looking up at me. "I didn't mean to fall asleep last night, but I was exhausted. I'm sorry if I disappointed you. I know you had certain expectations."

"That's bullshit. I care more about you getting the rest you need than sucking me off."

Adam ducked his head. "But that's what you're

paying me for. To entertain your clients and warm your bed."

"Adam, look at me." My fingers cupped his chin, tilting his face to meet mine. "What if it was more than that?"

"What do you mean?" His beautiful eyes shined bluer than the ocean outside our window.

"I'll show you, come with me." I pulled up my briefs and tugged Adam from the bed. I held my hands over his eyes, and he covered them with his hands and laughed while I led him down the hall and out to the living room.

"What are you doing?" He tried to tug my fingers apart so he could peek. "I can't walk around in my underwear when we have guests."

"They left early this morning. Lillian said she'll be in touch. Keep your eyes closed." When I wrangled him into position, I whispered excitedly in his ear. "Okay, open your eyes."

The look of astonishment on Adam's face chased by pure delight was worth every hour I'd spent preparing his surprise. The tree glittered in the morning sun. The tiny white lights reflected off the glass ornaments, creating a halo effect.

"A Christmas tree? Where did this come from?"

"A tree farm somewhere up north, I imagine." Adam spared me a look that said *obviously*. "Do you like it?"

"It's beautiful. And there are presents underneath."

"Merry Christmas, Adam." I stared at him as he studied the tree, completely oblivious to the somersaults my heart was doing in my chest.

"It's amazing to me. All you have to do is snap your fingers and a Christmas tree appears, fully decked out with lights, ornaments, and presents."

I trailed my lips across the back of his neck, making him shiver. "There's a little more to it than that."

Adam turned and slid his arms around my neck. "I love it."

"Then it was worth every hour I spent not sleeping last night."

The surprise on his face was evident. "You did all this? But why?"

My throat bobbed as I swallowed. "In case this was our first Christmas and not just our only Christmas." I led him over to the couch. "Adam, I told you I'm going to be here for the next two days, and I asked you to stay with me."

He nodded, his eyebrows scrunched together in confusion. "And I told you I would."

"I know you did. But that was before you had all the facts. If you stay, I'm not going to pay you for your time. There will be no entertaining clients and having sex with me because I'm paying you to. If you agree to stay, it will be because you *want* to be here with me. Desire, not obligation, Adam. Do you understand what I'm asking you for?"

He took my hands in his and squeezed them. "I do understand, and my answer is still yes. I don't want your money. I'd rather have you truly want me with you. It's a much more satisfying feeling. And I never slept with you just because you paid me to. You know how much I wanted it."

The vice that gripped my heart unfurled and the blood began to pump again as I took my first deep but hesitant breath. "Do you mean it? Is that really what you want? Because I could give you everything you dream of if you just take a chance on me."

His beautiful, tanned face relaxed. "It's the way you look at me like you're hungry. How you ask consent before you try to dominate me. And the way you take charge of my body when we have sex. You make me feel things I didn't know that I could, and you make me want things I didn't know I should. I see you when you're watching me, when you think you're unobserved. Something about me fascinates you and I hope you never lose that. I'm addicted to it. You listen, and you study me, and you're attracted to my body *and* my personality. The way you act toward me, you make me feel complete. I would be an idiot to walk away from that. And I'm not an idiot, Jones."

"I never thought you were."

Adam scooted onto my lap, parting his thighs over my hips. "I didn't think what you're offering was realistic. I mean, don't get me wrong, when I first met you, I thought you were a real..."

"Ass?"

He nodded, smirking. "And this is all so..."

"Sudden?"

"Exactly. And no matter how you look at me or touch me, it doesn't negate the fact that you are still an elitist snob and a bit of a dick. But you've shown me a softer side of you, and I don't want to walk away from that."

"I don't want you to, either." I sucked tiny open-mouth kisses across his smooth chest.

Adam tipped backward and viewed the tree upside down, smiling like a kid on Christmas morning. "Are the presents under the tree for me?"

My lips tipped into a smile. "Every one of them."

He straightened up and looked at me guiltily. "I didn't get you anything."

"Yes, you did, Adam." I placed his hand over my heart. "You gave me hope. I haven't smiled this much in years. Don't underestimate your gift. It's priceless."

Adam scooted off my lap and went over to sit on the floor by the tree. He fingered the beach-themed orna-ments, smiling as he admired the sand dollars and small starfish, glass seashells and colorful pieces of coral.

"This tree is so beautiful. It's perfect for this condo. Reminds me of my love of surfing and the beach."

He turned his attention to the presents and chose a medium-sized box wrapped in gold foil. I laughed as he shook the box, holding it to his ear as he tried to guess what might be inside.

"Just open it." I gestured impatiently.

He tore through the paper and opened the lid on the box. Adam looked curious as he lifted the book out of its tissue paper nest. He turned it over in his hands, inspecting the leather-bound covers before he flipped it open and thumbed through the blank pages.

"What is it?"

"A book." My sarcasm was met with a dubious look. "I know how much you love to cook, and I thought perhaps you'd like to teach me some of your skills. I was hoping we could fill the pages of the book with our own recipes that we create together."

Adam's eyes glistened with unshed tears as he crawled over to my lap and laid his head on my thighs. "Thank you. It's perfect."

I carded my fingers through his silky blond hair, in love with his reaction to the gift. "You're perfect. Go see what else is waiting for you under the tree."

He kissed each of my knees before returning to his spot. The next gift he picked up was a smaller box wrapped in red and black Buffalo check paper. After removing the silver bow, Adam tore through the paper and opened the box to reveal two printed tickets. I studied the changes in his face as he realized what he was looking at. His expression morphed from curiosity, to pleasure, to excitement. His bright eyes filled with awe as he gazed at me, speechless.

"No, you didn't!"

"I most certainly did."

Satisfaction warmed my body. If I had any doubts that we were moving too fast, this laid those thoughts to rest. Obviously, I knew Adam better than I thought I did because my gifts hit the nail on the head.

"Season tickets with box seats at the Performing Arts Center? This is too much, Jones! These tickets had to cost a fortune."

"In case you hadn't noticed, I have a few dollars to

spare. And now you'll never miss another show. We'll be front and center for every one of them."

The smile on his face was worth every penny I spent. How silly of Adam to think he hadn't given me any gifts. The gratification I felt from seeing his delight and knowing I was the source of it was all the gift I needed.

"Also, that brand new wetsuit you wore snorkeling yesterday is yours to keep for surfing." His manic joy over the theater tickets mellowed into a contented smile. "I believe you have one more gift under the tree."

Adam reached for the red envelope propped at the base of the tree and broke the seal to retrieve the card inside. "A gift card to a home decor store? You haven't even seen the inside of my apartment yet, but I assure you, it's not that bad."

His wrong assumption made me laugh. "It's not for your apartment, it's for my penthouse. It's cold and sterile, and it lacks the warmth it needs to feel like a home. I'm hoping to remedy that in two ways. The first is that you move in with me. And the second is that you use this gift card to buy things you like to make it feel more like *your* home."

"You don't do anything halfway, do you?" He smirked as he crawled back over to my lap again. This time, he climbed up and straddled my legs. Adam twined his arms around my neck and brushed his nose against mine. "Are you asking me to stay often?"

"Don't play coy with me. I'm asking you to move in. I don't want to hear your protests about how it's too soon. I learned in business that if something feels right, you should trust your instincts. Everything about you feels right, Adam. And every time I trust my instincts where it concerns you, I'm never disappointed."

"You know, now that I think of it, I just remembered I do have a present for you to open. But I left it in the bedroom. Follow me." The heat in his sapphire eyes told me exactly what he had in mind.

He shook his perfect ass as he walked down the hall, and I had no choice but to follow. I'd follow that ass off a cliff.

CHAPTER 16
ADAM

Two glorious days alone with Jones without work, meetings, or clients. Zero distractions. Just him and me and another sunny day aboard his boat.

I felt as if I was living someone else's life. What started out as a one night stand turned into a torrid affair, and then he asked me to move in with him. Jones was making long-term plans for our future and moving at a pace that was making my head swim. That was how he worked, swift and decisive. It had worked for him in business, and I was trusting that it would work for us.

He offered everything that I ever wanted on a silver platter, and I was afraid of reaching for it and having it turn into a mirage. A decoy of the perfect relationship I'd dreamed of at night alone in my bed.

We had a lot to discuss about moving forward together, but despite our opposite personalities, we always seemed to be on the same page.

Jones handed me a fishing pole. He nestled up behind me and wrapped his arms around me as he instructed me how to work the reel. I didn't have much experience with fishing, and at the moment, I only cared about his heat on my back and his bulge pressed into the crease of my ass.

My attraction to him was spinning out of control. Just thinking of him made me hard.

"Press this button lightly and ease the rod back over your shoulder. Then, flick it forward smoothly and release the button." His warm breath tickled my ear, sending ripples of lust down my spine.

I copied his instructions and watched as my line sailed through the air and landed in the water with a plunk. "Are we going to eat what we catch?"

Jones chuckled rich and deep. "I don't filet fish, I order it in a restaurant." He placed his hands over mine and together, we reeled my line back in. "If you're in the mood for fish, I'll take you to any seafood restaurant you choose."

God, the way he spoiled me. I'd never get used to it.

After an hour of fishing, we ended up in the sunroom to avoid the chilly December wind. Sunshine streamed through the windows and warmed the small salon. Jones poured drinks for us as I stripped out of my clothes. When he turned from the wet bar, he laughed with surprise.

"Is it too hot in here for you?"

"It's about to be too hot in here for *you*."

There was no way I was getting off of this boat

without fulfilling my fantasy of being fucked in front of these windows. When I was fully naked, I sat on the sofa and spread my thighs, providing Jones with a peek of my hole. He carried my drink over to me and set it down on the table next to my arm. Then, he sat across from me and reclined as he sipped his scotch, enjoying the show. His teasing eyes dared me to seduce him.

I reached into the glass at my elbow and retrieved an ice cube. After sucking it between my lips, I trailed it down my chest and stomach to my groin. Jones's eyes tracked the movement like a lion stalking its prey. I teased my hard cock with the ice cube, running it down the length of my shaft. Chilly drops of water dripped over my sac and ran down my crease. My fingers spread the water around my hole. The cold liquid made it quiver, and Jones groaned as I dipped my finger inside. He downed the rest of his drink in one shot and licked his lips clean before dropping to his knees in front of me.

His tongue licked around my finger and caressed my rim. The added wetness of his saliva helped my finger glide deeper. Then, his finger joined mine as he stretched me wider. Whimpering from the burn, I worked my ass over our fingers, taking them deeper as Jones's wicked tongue continued to lick me.

He growled as he worked his shorts down his long legs. "You started this, not me. But I'm going to finish it how I see fit. You've got me so worked up, there's no way I can be gentle with you. By the time I'm done with you, your ass is going to hurt for the next two days. Let that be a lesson to you about provoking me," he growled, sounding like a man possessed.

His warning sent a thrill of anticipation shooting through me, and I couldn't wait for him to devour me. He slipped his finger from me, and I felt empty with the loss. I turned over and kneeled facing the back of the couch, presenting my ass to him, but he roughly gripped my hips.

"We're going to do this my way, not yours." Jones licked a stripe up my spine, and when he reached my shoulder, he sank his teeth deep into the bunched muscle. I hissed from the bite, and he slapped my ass cheek. "Go stand by the window and rest your hands on it. You wanted to put on a show, so that's what we're going to do. We'll give everyone that passes by something to see."

We were fairly close to the Harbor, which meant there was a considerable amount of boat traffic outside the windows. The idea that we might be spotted by someone sent a jolt of lust straight to my cock. I'd never entertained the idea of voyeurism and exhibitionism before now, but when I saw this room, it was the first thing that came to mind.

I braced my hands against the window and popped my ass, legs spread. Jones dragged his lubed finger through my crease. When I glanced back, I saw him stroke his cock as he slicked it. He looked incredibly sexy touching himself like that, slow and deliberate. Sliding his hand down to the base, he gripped his shaft and lined himself up with my hole. His fingers dug into my hips and held me steady as he pushed inside my body with a deep grunt.

I whined from the pleasure and pain of his thickness splitting me wide open. He felt incredible as he buried himself deep inside of me. Jones reached up to grab my throat with one hand while the other continued to steady my hips as he thrust into me. His body thundered against mine in a wild rhythm and the slap of our skin echoed through the empty room. The head of his cock was hitting incredibly deep within me, and I shouted his name with an uninhibited cry of satisfaction.

He stilled, probably to stave off his orgasm. He panted harshly in my ear. "I'm going to stay very still while you fuck yourself on my cock." His big palm slapped my ass cheek, stinging my sweaty skin. "If you want it, come and get it." I nearly came from his words and the suggestion that he was urging me to act like a total slut. "Work that ass for me, baby."

I wiggled and worked, sheathing him in my tight heat until I felt his dick pulse and kick inside of me. I clenched my muscles around his thick girth and milked his cock as he came deep inside my body.

And that was when I realized he wasn't wearing a condom. I was so worked up when we began that it slipped my mind, and I wondered if that was what happened to him as well.

Or was it deliberate?

Jones reached around my hips and gripped my leaking dick. He pumped me four times before I shot onto the thick glass in front of me with a desperate cry. I collapsed against the window as deep shuddering breaths heaved from my chest. My legs felt boneless like jelly, and my shoulders ached from holding myself up against the impact of Jones's powerful body slamming into me. My heart raced from adrenaline and a spike of anxiety.

I had to ask why he did it.

Jones knelt and spread my cheeks. His warm wet tongue licked around my hole before delving inside to catch the remnants of his seed that threatened to drip down my crease. No one had ever eaten me out after coming inside of me before. Until now, it was only something I'd seen in porn. The act felt beyond intimate, and I was convinced that any man who would clean and care for me this way after using my body meant me no harm.

If it was deliberate, he had his reasons, and I realized in that moment that I trusted Jones completely.

His lips sealed around my pucker, and I felt the gentle pulling suction as his mouth drained every bit of the mess from my hole. When he stood, he pulled me into his arms, and I melted into his broad chest. His mouth hovered over mine, seeking permission to kiss me. My lips parted and my tongue snaked inside his mouth, feeding from the bitter sweetness that coated his tongue. Jones moaned into my mouth, kissing me with desperate fervor.

Would I ever get used to his appetite for me?

He guided me to the couch and when we sat, Jones tucked me into his side and wrapped his strong arms around me. "Something is wrong. You're too quiet."

With my head against his chest, the vibration of the deep rumble of his voice as he talked soothed me, and I nestled deeper.

"You didn't use a condom." It wasn't so much a question as a statement.

"No, *we* didn't use a condom. We are two consenting adults, and we are both responsible for our actions. Before I entered you, you watched me stroke myself and you saw that I wore no condom. We should definitely have discussed it beforehand, but it just—"

"Happened. Too quickly." I lifted my eyes to his face, and he cupped my jaw. His thumb stroked over my cheekbone as he gazed into my eyes.

"I thought about it for a split second before I acted. Adam, I trust you completely and know that you would never have sex with me if you knew that you were positive and hadn't talked to me about it first. I know you test yourself regularly, and I'm convinced you would have shared those results with me if you had something to tell me. You know that I test myself often because I sleep with the escorts that I hire without knowing their history. I would never have done that if I thought I was jeopardizing your safety."

"I believe that, too. I trust you completely and I appreciate that you trust me as well. But the next time we come across an important situation, let's talk about it first like adults."

He smiled ruefully. "Cross my heart."

Jones captured my lips again in a sweetly affirming kiss. The quickly progressive pace of our relationship left me with many niggling reservations, but I could cross trust and honesty off of my list.

"Let me take you to dinner. Let's get cleaned up first, then you can choose anywhere in the city you'd like me to take you."

THE MEXICAN RESTAURANT I chose wasn't what Jones had in mind for our first official restaurant date. He probably thought I'd choose a swanky steakhouse or expensive seafood restaurant by the water. Though I enjoyed nice things, a casual dining experience was more my style.

Jones grimaced as he looked over his choices. "This menu is sticky."

I tried to cover my smile by holding my menu in front of my face, but there was no hiding my laughter from him.

"What?" He looked genuinely confused.

"Nothing, I find you adorably attractive when you act like a snob."

"Is that a nice way of saying I'm an asshole?" Jones was caught between laughing at himself and scowling at me.

Laughter bubbled from my throat. "In the nicest possible way, yes."

A commotion to my left drew my attention. "Oh my God! Would you look at who it is? Fancy running into the two of you here." Marianne approached our table with several other wives in tow.

I pasted a bright smile on my face and greeted the ladies. "Is it? I don't believe in coincidences."

Jones acted like an ambassador, employing his impeccable manners and good breeding. "Good evening, ladies. What brings you to a fine dining establishment such as this one on a Monday?"

Susan tittered. "It's margarita Monday, Jones. The ladies always meet for margaritas on Mondays. Maybe next time Adam can join us. If he's not busy." She pointed a look at me, and I smirked.

"And you didn't invite me because you just guessed that I was busy? Or because you were spying on me with binoculars and saw that we left the condo, and then called Amanda to find out where we were headed."

Marianne had the grace to blush, and Jones looked horrified. "Seriously?" He looked at me in question. "How do you know they do that?"

My eyebrow arched and half of my mouth tipped up in a sarcastic smirk. "How many times do I have to tell you? Don't underestimate the Executive Wives Club." Turning back to Marianne and Susan, I warned, "I hope you ladies are enjoying the show we've been putting on, but if I find any of those pictures online, I will feed you those binoculars piece by piece."

Jones gasped. "Are they seriously watching us in the bedroom?"

"In the bedroom, the living room, the balcony, and I wouldn't doubt they followed us to the boat." I leveled my stare on the wives, their guilty and inflamed expressions told me they'd seen plenty.

Jones recovered his cool demeanor. "I'll be sending Amanda by tomorrow to collect those binoculars."

I laughed as I studied my menu. "Don't bother. She's in on it, too."

The ladies dissolved into laughter and waved good-bye. When I looked up, Jones's eyes bugged out of his head. "*My* Amanda?"

The silent laughter that shook my shoulders was all the answer he needed.

"You know, I've been going about things all wrong. You're absolutely correct, I underestimated the wives, but I won't make that mistake again. They're running the show, aren't they?"

I looked at Jones as if he were a toddler. "You finally get it. I know that you think your big fancy degrees and cunning business skills make you superior to the charitable volunteer lunch set, but I promise you those ladies are responsible for the position their husbands have in your company. Those men could never get where they are without the imagination and ambitious drive of their wives."

Jones was silent as he considered the truth behind my observation. "The next time we entertain clients, I'm putting the wives to work. If I can get them to win over my client's partner, then we have a better chance of landing the account, don't we?"

"Of course. Didn't you see how I handled Lillian Manson?"

Our waitress approached and took our orders. We

shared a sizzling skillet of shrimp fajitas and ordered margaritas.

"It's you," Jones said between bites. "I know how to invest money, but you know how to invest in people. You are warm and genuine, and people are attracted to your goodness. You draw people to you like a moth to a flame—myself included."

A wicked grin spread across my lips. "I bet you ten bucks they leave as soon as they see us ask for the check. The EWC is going to make good use of the binoculars before you take them away tomorrow."

Jones laughed. His foot brushed mine under the table. "Drink up. I want you loose so we can put on a good show."

CHAPTER 17
JONES

The following evening, we headed back to the city. No sooner had we settled in before Amanda stopped by with an arm full of presents and a pair of binoculars.

"Welcome home, handsome." Her heels clicked over the tiled floor as she made her way toward the living room.

"Thank you, I think?"

Amanda laughed as she brushed by me. "I was talking to Adam. Here, these are for you." She dumped the presents at his feet and passed him the binoculars.

"How do I know you didn't buy these on the way here? I bet good money that the EWC is still in possession of their high-powered binoculars." He held them up to his eyes, and I assumed he was testing their strength.

Amanda playfully swatted his chest. "Don't be so cynical. I think Jones is starting to wear off on you."

Adam gestured toward the pile at his feet. "Who are all of these from?"

"Your fan club. And the little one on top is from me. The ladies of the Executive Wives Club send their regards, as did the clients you've met so far."

"Did I get anything?" I felt silly asking, but seriously, Adam had been in my life less than two weeks. How did he become so popular so quickly?

"I think they sent you a bag of coal." Amanda and Adam laughed at her sarcasm.

"Next week, I'll have a moving company deliver your stuff from your apartment. It was difficult to find anyone on such short notice during the holiday." She bent to press a kiss to Adam's cheek. "Merry Christmas, Happy New Year, and welcome home. I'll get out of your hair now so you can celebrate."

Adam walked her to the door and locked it behind her. When he rejoined me in the living room, he laughed at my pout. "Aw, don't feel bad, Scrooge. Would you like to open some of my presents?"

I struggled not to roll my eyes and moved to the couch. "The only present I want to open is in your pants. But before we get to the fun and games, I'd like to talk to you about something important." Adam made himself comfortable beside me, giving me his full attention. "I know you are on break from school for the holiday, and when you return, you'll only be there a short while before the semester ends. We haven't talked about your plans for work after you move in here, but I assume you aren't going to escort any longer. I would really like for you to just focus on school next semester and let me worry about everything else."

Adam breathed out a long heavy breath as he ran his fingers through his hair. "Of course I'm not going to continue to escort. But there are other things that I can do for work. I don't expect you to pay my way through life."

My frank expression said that I was all business. "I'm not interested in entertaining your misplaced notions about equality and gender roles within a committed relationship. I told you that I'm not keen on being your sugar daddy. But that doesn't mean that I can't float us financially until you begin your career. There's nothing wrong with taking it easy while you finish school and make it your first priority."

He looked conflicted as I took his hands in mine and squeezed. It was the perfect moment to swoop in and seal the deal. "Let me take care of you, Adam. Don't you see? It makes me feel good to provide for you. It doesn't mean that you're taking advantage or using me. You are allowing me to care for you with actions instead of words, and that means so much to me."

"So this is one of your dominating control freak things?" Adam looked faintly amused and suspiciously skeptical.

"Something like that." My hand cut through the air as I waved him off. "Do we need to label it?"

"You are incredibly high-handed. Do you always get your way?"

My lips caressed his knuckles. "When it comes to you, I hope so."

~

"WHAT ARE our plans this evening? I'd kill to order some Thai food and watch a movie together."

When Adam found me, I was standing in my closet, choosing something to wear for the evening. His suggestion sounded heavenly, but—obligations.

"We're headed back out to the marina tonight." I almost laughed when his face fell dramatically. "We're meeting my partners and their wives aboard the boat for the annual Festival of Boats Parade."

He brightened, but only slightly. "They feature it on the news every year, but I've never seen it in person."

"It's actually pretty spectacular. Hopefully, you won't be disappointed." Adam sidled up next to me and fingered my shirts hanging on the rod. Looking at them arranged by color and all facing the same way made me realize I might have a touch of OCD. "Do we need to run by your apartment to grab a change of clothes? Or we could go out and buy something new."

His face soured when I mentioned shopping. "What am I expected to wear?"

"Business casual. Perhaps more casual and less business. It's going to be cool and windy out, so keep that in mind."

Adam reached around me and unzipped my pants. "Show me what you plan to wear, and I'll dress you."

His smoky voice in my ear and the seductive vision he put in my head made my cock instantly hard under his hand. "I may not fit in my pants if you keep this up."

"I can remedy that, as well."

He reached into my pants and pulled my cock out. As he stroked my length, I pushed back against him to find him just as hard. "Adam," I groaned. "As much as I want to see where this leads, we can't be late."

His quiet chuckle teased my ear. "As long as you promise me one thing. When we're sitting in the salon tonight, I want you to remember how you fucked me in front of that window. And when we're out on the deck, I want you to remember how I wrapped my lips around your cock while you fished."

"Like I could forget." I shucked my pants and reached for his. "Fuck my partners. Let's be late."

THE STIFF WIND that blew in off the water had a distinct bite. I was grateful for my sweater, a black cashmere V-neck that I paired with burgundy pants. Adam borrowed a black cable-knit that he combined with charcoal pants. He looked sinfully sexy in the fitted slacks and sharp sweater. It made my fingers itch to undress him.

We were the last to arrive, to no one's surprise. The ladies greeted us with knowing smiles and pointed us in the direction of the liquor. As I poured Adam's drink, the wives immediately surrounded him, and I knew I'd lost him for the next hour or so. He accepted the drink and winked charmingly before I disappeared in search of my partners. I envied him that he would have all the fun tonight while I bided my time until we could return home.

As I stood at the rail on deck and sipped the scotch in my glass, I looked out over the dark water and contemplated how good it felt to be the luckiest man alive. I might have used my impeccable judgment and solid instincts to single Adam out as a good thing, but his decision to accept me and return my affection was a twist of fate I hadn't planned for. Now that he had agreed to move in with me, I wouldn't slow down. It was full steam ahead toward our bright future.

I was going to make Adam's dreams come true, just as he had already seen to mine.

CHAPTER 18
ADAM

Becoming an honorary member of the EWC was more enjoyable than I could have imagined. Marianne, Susan, and the other wives treated me with genuine affection and offered their friendship easily and without reservation. They were a fun group of women and we seemed to have quite a bit in common, despite the fact that we ran in different social circles.

As I sipped my second cranberry martini, Kimberly regaled me with the events of her long ago engagement. All of the ladies seemed to have matrimony on their minds as they projected their dreams of my future with Jones into every conversation.

"I was the girl his parents wanted him to marry, and when he realized he actually liked me, he dropped to his knees."

That made me chuckle. "Yeah, that means something different to gay men."

All the ladies laughed as Kimberly clarified. "He

proposed, you wicked man. And it happens to mean the same thing to women. It's exactly what he did after he slid the ring on my finger."

It was a visual I didn't need or want, but I dutifully laughed along with everyone else. Thankfully, we were interrupted by the blast of an air horn in the distance that signaled the parade was underway. I saved Jones a spot beside me at the rail, and when I felt him cozy up to my side, I melted into his embrace as he slipped his arm around my shoulders. The heat from his body warmed me and he felt like home.

It amazed me that this abrasive, incredible man could find a place in my heart in such a short time. But when I thought of a future with him, I had no more reservations. I was all in.

We pointed at the spectacle of boats that sailed past in a procession of colorful lights. Familiar holiday music blared from speakers and filled the harbor with the festive sounds of Christmas.

Although being on this yacht among these people was a million miles away from the daily routine of my usual life, I felt like I belonged. It had everything to do with Jones's love and acceptance. With the added bonus of the warm and welcoming wives, I could see many more memories made with this found family that had adopted me so eagerly.

∾

THE HOME DECOR store was packed with shoppers looking for an after-Christmas bargain. Jones insisted we spend my gift card today. I believe he was hedging his bets to ensure that I didn't change my mind about moving in. He wanted my mark on every surface of his penthouse—*our penthouse.*

God, that sounded weird. Would I ever get used to feeling like everything he surrounded me with was partly mine? Probably not, since I hadn't earned it. But that didn't seem to matter to Jones. He gave everything he had achieved freely to me in hopes that I would make a home for us.

In an effort to level the playing field between us, and because I couldn't resist screwing with him, I paid extra attention to every mermaid chachki we passed. When Jones caught on, he pretended to avert his eyes whenever we approached another display with mermaid themed items. He hoped that I would bypass it if he didn't look interested, but no such luck.

"Wow!" I exclaimed as I touched a particularly gaudy mermaid covered in green and gold glitter. Jones's eyes widened in horror as he imagined the tacky mermaid adorning his bathroom counter. "I just can't pass up a cute mermaid. I have an affinity for them."

It was all I could do to swallow my laughter as a shudder of revulsion rippled down Jones's spine. It was the final test that he was crazy about me as he allowed me to place the ugly figurine in our basket without saying a word. I added three more, each one bigger and bolder than the last, before he finally excused himself to go to the bathroom. When he returned, I was doubled over the side of the cart in laughter.

Jones spied the empty cart with confused relief.

"Where are your nautical friends?"

His attempt to be politically correct about ugly mermaids made me laugh even harder. I twined my arms around his waist and smothered my laughter into his chest. Jones stroked my back. He probably assumed I was having a minor meltdown.

"I'm fucking with you. I don't have any obsession with mermaids. They were God awful and I specifically chose them to make you scared to have me move in."

Jones waited for my laughter to subside as he regarded me with an amused, indulgent grin. "I don't care what you bring home today. Nothing is going to make me afraid to have you move in with me. I want it more than anything."

When his lips brushed mine, I fell a little harder for him.

In the end, I chose a soft throw blanket that looked like it was dyed in bold watercolor paint splotches, a lamp made of glass and driftwood, several scented candles, colorful patterned throw pillows that reminded me of the ones at the beach house, and a sprig of plastic mistletoe from the Christmas clearance table. Jones questioned the mistletoe, but I had my reasons.

"Mistletoe? I don't need a reason or a reminder to kiss you. I'll gladly do it whenever." To prove his point, he captured my lips in a slow, sweet kiss that turned all of the curious eyes in the checkout line on us.

~

OVER THE NEXT TWO DAYS, the mistletoe turned up everywhere. I surprised him with it every chance I got. When he was taking a shower, I snuck into the steamy glass enclosure, holding the mistletoe. Jones used conditioner for lube and fucked me against the wall.

When Jones was on a phone call with a client, I snuck up behind him, tossed the mistletoe onto his desk, and spun his chair around. I dropped to my knees for him and wished him a merry Christmas with my mouth.

Jones invited me to have a drink with him on the balcony. I pulled the mistletoe from my pocket and teased it down his chest and over the obvious bulge in his pants. He coated my hole with ice from his drink and bent me over the railing before he railed me.

The mistletoe turned out to be the best two dollars I'd ever spent. Jones agreed that it was a sound investment, as he usually reaped the benefits and rewards. On my way to the bathroom to brush my teeth this morning, he jumped out of the closet as I passed by and snagged my arm, pulling me inside. He dangled the mistletoe over my head, his naughty laugh warned me he was about to drop to his knees. Jones pulled down my cotton sleep pants and swallowed me whole as he hummed *We Wish You A Merry Christma* around my cock.

My phone vibrated with a text alert. When I checked it, I groaned. "Fuck me."

Jones looked up from his newspaper. "I did, this morning. Would you like to go again?"

"No, I mean, yes, but no. It's my friends. They're back in town and they're throwing a New Year's Eve party tonight. They want us to attend. Well, me. They don't know about you yet, but they suspect. Griffin told me to bring my *new friend*. That would be you."

"Okay, so we'll go. How bad can it be?" Jones laughed when I palmed my face. "What should I wear to this shindig?"

Jones's wire-rimmed reading glasses highlighted the blue in his eyes—with his legs crossed over the knee and the newspaper in hand, he looked refined and studious —I wanted to dirty him up.

"They're planning to gather at that fancy new bar that opened recently, Limericks Lounge. I think my friends, Murphy and Hudson, wore out their welcome at the old Limericks Bar and Grille, and they mean to invade the new lounge and mark their territory. *If* they can get past the front door, that is."

He laid his paper across his knee and removed his glasses. "How do you wear out your welcome at a bar?"

"I'm not exactly sure, but I've heard stories, and they're quite entertaining. But then again, where Murphy is involved, nothing surprises me."

Jones shoved to his feet and joined me at the island where he laid his paper down. He kissed my clean-shaven cheek, regarding me with amusement.

"Well, I think I have the right kind of clothes for a party in an upscale dinner club. Don't worry, I'll try my best not to embarrass you in front of your friends."

Not likely. "It's not you, it's them. You have to keep in

mind my friends are young and dumb. It's not really your crowd." Would meeting my friends highlight the differences between Jones and me?

He laid my fears to rest with a kiss. "If you like them and they matter to you, then I'll make it my crowd because *you* matter to *me*."

CHAPTER 19

JONES

T otal lie. I couldn't care less about spending the evening with a bunch of college escorts. More than likely, I had nothing in common with these men. Except Adam. That was the only reason I needed to get dressed and show up. However, I was more than a little interested in checking out the new lounge. Talk about the swanky establishment had circled the office, was overheard by Amanda and then imparted to me. It was good to be in the know in case I chose to take my clients there.

ADAM LOOKED EFFORTLESSLY stunning in a fitted black cashmere V-neck sweater and tailored black trousers, sophisticated yet sexy. His tanned chest peeked from the neck of his sweater and when we stepped outside, the chilly air hardened his nipples, visible through the thin cashmere. The reminder of his hard, toned body gave me second thoughts about staying home and celebrating the new year in our bed with a bottle of champagne. Everything about him teased my senses and made me hungry to use him to whet my appetite.

Adam brushed by me as I held the door open, his smoky citrus scent seduced me. I wanted to pull him into my arms and breathe deeply to sate my craving for him.

It satisfied me to see the rainbow sticker on the glass doors that denoted this was a queer friendly establishment. Several businesses around town had displayed them more often lately, and I hoped it would be a trend that continued to spread. The dim interior of the lounge beckoned me with music and warmer air, and I followed Adam inside.

The atmosphere was elegant—understated, yet comfortable. Limericks Lounge was the kind of place I could loosen my tie and relax with a good quality bourbon after work. A group of young men gathered near the bar waved us over. They were deep in conversation with the bartender, a striking man in his thirties with black hair and icy blue eyes, much like myself.

The men greeted Adam warmly with hugs and backslaps. Even in my twenties in college, I couldn't recall having a group of friends like this. Adam would say it was because I had a stick up my ass. The thought made me smile to myself. He somehow appreciated me in spite of my antisocial and judgmental ways. I caught the tail end of their conversation as I joined their group.

A man with a face full of freckles and fiery red hair

leaned over the bar. "What happened, Shannon? Murphy drove away all of your customers at the bar, so you had to open a new place?"

"Something like that." The man named Shannon stopped polishing the glass in his hand and looked around nervously, his blue eyes darting left and right past the doors. "He's not coming, is he?"

The man with red hair laughed. His smile was pure trouble. "Should be here any minute."

The bartender, his expression ominous, smacked the sparkling glass down on the counter, banging it loudly against the dark granite bartop. "As long as Hudson keeps a tight leash on him, he can stay."

"Don't worry. Hudson loves to tighten Murphy's leash." They all laughed, reminding me I wasn't privy to the inside joke because I was the stranger...the outcast... the new guy.

As if on cue, they all turned to me with interest, eyeing me like a starving man looks at a piece of meat on a buffet. "And who are you? A *friend* of Adam's?"

I didn't miss the way he emphasized the word friend. "Jones Marin. Pleasure to meet you." I stuck my hand out to shake but was quickly pulled into a hug.

"Any friend of Adam's is a friend of mine." The redhead clapped my back like he had done to Adam, initiating me into their tight circle of friends without a second thought.

A short, cute twink with coppery curls and the greenest eyes nudged him aside. "You don't happen to live out by the beach, do you?" Several of the men looked interested in my answer, and I had to wonder what Adam might have said about me in my absence.

Adam jumped into the fray to rescue me, which I found endearing. Was my self-assured, sexy boyfriend, who never backed down from a challenge, suddenly nervous around this group?

"So, while you were in Vermont for the holidays, I answered a call that changed my life. I'm going to skip past all the juicy details and get to the bottom line. I moved in with Jones recently. Things are serious and we're happy. Also, I won't be escorting any longer. I'm sorry if that leaves you in the lurch, Lucky."

Lucky assessed us silently. I could see the gears turning in his head as he came to his own conclusions. I hoped for Adam's sake that he didn't give him a hard time because I would need to intervene, and I promised Adam I would be on my best behavior.

But instead, he smiled and pulled Adam in for another hug. "Nobody understands your position better than me. I knew on the first date that Hayes was the last man I would ever sleep with. When you know, you know."

"Same," said the tall brunet at his side. "When Griffin hired me to—let's just say I knew on our first date–if you can call it a date–that he was the one."

"The first night I laid in Reid's bed, I was done for," said a tall stocky blond man. He stuck his hand in my face. "I'm Riley. This is my husband, Reid. Nice to meet you. Adam has told us absolutely nothing about you, so don't mind our nosy questions."

The bartender, Shannon, tossed a terry cloth rag over his shoulder and shook his head, laughing, the sound rich and deep. "Go make yourselves comfortable in the lounge and I'll send one of my cousins over to take your orders." Shannon gestured toward the open seating area opposite the bar.

The lounge had intimate groupings of small and larger tables and leather booths that invited intimate conversations and long hours sipping cocktails or enjoying a fine dinner. A large stage encompassed one end of the room where a man dressed in a tuxedo sat at a black baby grand piano. His fingers moved nimbly over the ivory keys as he produced the sweetest sounds that filled the room with mellow jazz.

We chose a large table off to the side of the room and I didn't miss that his friends strategically placed us in the center so they could attack us from all sides with pointed questions. It was a brilliant strategy designed to break me down and get me to spill our secrets. But I was a master strategist, a cunning businessman. They would get nothing from me but vague answers and polite smiles.

Just as we sat, a couple joined us, the taller man resembled a blond viking and bore a striking resemblance to Hayes. The smaller man had the identical fiery red hair and freckles as Lucky. They introduced themselves as Hudson and Murphy, the latter man eyed me curiously.

Our server approached the table dressed in a white button-down and black vest with matching pants that showed off his trim figure. His dark hair and bright green eyes drew my attention. Just because I was head over heels about the man sitting next to me didn't mean I couldn't appreciate beauty in others. It seemed I wasn't the only one who noticed his good looks, as Adam's eyes mapped his features as if he were studying for an exam.

"Good evening, gentlemen. Welcome to Limericks Lounge. For those of you that don't know me, my name is Carson, and I'll be your server this evening. For those of you that do know me, keep in mind I'm working a holiday and I know who you are, so tip your server well."

His enigmatic smile transformed his chiseled face from sultry to charming, revealing a delicious dimple. He winked at those he knew, flashing those pretty green eyes to just about everyone but me and Adam.

Yeah, over my cold, dead, and lifeless body was Adam coming back here without me to drink with the sexy server. I'd somehow managed to snag the hottest, kindest, smartest guy in town, and I wouldn't chance losing him to Carson the cutie or any other young buck. Not only was I considerably older than these guys, I was out of touch with their generation. I lived in a different world. In some ways, that gave me an advantage over them, and in some ways, it left me the odd man out.

But I'd be damned if I gave them any leverage over my weaknesses. What I needed was a solid plan to ensure a level playing field. I couldn't risk letting Adam get away. He's *mine*. He was meant for *me*, and I'd make sure he never regretted that. What I needed was to formulate a contract and get him to sign on the dotted line. And I had the perfect idea. My fingers ghosted over Adam's thigh. His hand covered mine with a reassuring squeeze, and the thought forming in my mind suddenly became crystal clear.

Nothing had ever felt so right.

When Carson returned with our drinks, I made sure to keep Adam's glass filled the entire night. I got to know more about his friends by sitting quietly and listening to everything said and unsaid. I would never possess Adam's kind and generous nature. To me, life was a game and people were pieces on a chessboard to be played to my advantage. With the largest goal of my life looming ahead, I could leave nothing to chance—I had to get this right. That meant, learning the ins and outs of navigating his social scene, his family dynamic, and his innermost desires.

In order to master the nuances of his personality, I needed to know his wildest fantasies, his most secret hopes and dreams. Did they align with mine? Were we on the same page when it came to our future? God, I hoped so because I was betting everything on his answer.

Around ten o'clock, the piano player wrapped up his talented performance with a bow and exited the stage to light applause. The lighting and music changed as more people drifted away from the bar to gather in the lounge. The main attraction was about to begin. Adam flashed his glassy, bright blue eyes at me, his beautiful face flushed with excitement. He was enjoying himself and I was loath to end his good time, but I was also determined to be inside of him when we rang in the new year in less than two hours from now.

A striking slender man of medium height sashayed onto the darkened stage wearing a short red satin robe. A single blue spotlight shone down on his short blond hair, casting shadows over the hard planes of his fine cheek-bones. He was a beautiful man, long toned legs plugged into sexy red stilettos swished gracefully as he moved. The silky robe was shed from his shoulders slowly, a seductive dance of satin and long limbs that made my mouth salivate to see what he wore beneath.

He wore sinful red lingerie, a matched set of delicate lace, and my cock hardened instantly when I imagined Adam wearing something similar. The thought never occurred to me until now, but it was my new favorite fantasy. He let the robe pool on the floor as he stepped over it, shaking his ass, on full display, with just a red string to part his creamy cheeks. His sexy burlesque dance caught the eye of every man and woman in atten-dance–he appealed to everyone. His enthusiastic routine was classically beautiful and breathtaking, as he flipped and split his long legs effortlessly. He made it look so easy, but I doubt it was anything but hours and hours of strenuous training and practice.

The pint-sized redhead with so much sass and personality addressed the group, his face hopeful but confident. "I think I could do that."

The big blond man seated beside him, Hudson, scoffed, eyes shining with amusement. "I'm sure you could, Fudgesicle. You can do anything you put your mind to. And I'd love to see you in that red lace set he's wearing."

The redhead, Murphy, looked skeptical. "Are you fucking with me? I can't tell." He surveyed the entire table, searching for the collective vibe. "Cause I'm really bendy, and I look great in red."

His partner, Hudson, smiled fondly at him and leaned in to nip his neck. "You might have to prove that to me later."

I liked Murphy instantly. He seemed like a fun ball of adventure. What appealed to me most was his sincerity and genuine personality. With a guy like that, what you saw was what you got. It was one of my favorite qualities in a person. I had no time for artifice and games. I much preferred someone to be upfront and honest about their intentions, save everyone a lot of time and money.

The sexy burlesque dancer continued the floor show for another hour until I tapped Adam's shoulder to gain his attention. My lips brushed over the shell of his ear, his eyes dilated, and a shiver rolled through his shoulders at the contact.

"Let me take you home. I want to celebrate midnight alone with you."

His face turned fully toward me, lips closing over mine, velvet tongue sliding into my mouth. His body was soft and pliant against mine, with not a hint of resistance as he melted into me.

"You can take me anywhere you want, we can celebrate anything tonight, as long as you take this off."

His fingers tugged at the buttons of my shirt. Adam

had definitely reached the limit of his alcohol intake. It was past time to head home. I urged him to his feet, bid his friends goodbye, and ushered him from the room. On our way out, I settled my tab at the bar with Shannon, and left the tab open for his friends, my treat. I wasn't above buying a good first impression.

Outside, the brisk night air nipped at our cheeks as we hustled to my car. Adam fidgeted with the radio as I drove. "Did you enjoy yourself?"

In an unexpected show of tenderness, Adam laid his head on my shoulder. "Mmm, very much. I like being your real date much better than your paid one."

Stifling my laughter, I kissed the top of his head. Alcohol seemed to make Adam's lips loose and his tongue honest. I highly approved.

CHAPTER 20
ADAM

My head swam pleasantly, a warm buzz flushed my body. I felt good—loose. Happy. Jones looked so hot tonight, so self-assured despite being the new guy in the hot seat. The way he sipped his drink, watched me surreptitiously from the corner of his eye, like a panther stalking his prey, lit a fire in my blood, turning it into liquid heat.

The hungry look in his pale eyes as he ushered me into our bedroom made my heart race. That look promised a night of sinful delights. Jones backed me up to the bed and undressed me with agonizing slowness, drawing out his treat. He intended to thoroughly devour me tonight, and I couldn't wait to be consumed by his ravenous appetite.

With my sweater removed, his possessive gaze roved over my chest, lingered on my tight nipples. Just having his undivided attention focused on me made my body hard all over.

"Touch your nipples, Adam."

I obeyed his command, teasing the hard nubs until they felt overstimulated and sensitive to my touch.

I ached to remove his shirt but knew better than to act without permission when he was this worked up, strung as tight as a clothesline. Jones wasn't feeling playful tonight. He was on a mission to seduce me, to own me completely. And he did, but I was smart enough not to let him know that.

This enigmatic man, who was once such a mystery, had become so familiar to me in the past several weeks, as familiar as my own name. His complex personality hid his soft heart, a razor-sharp wit and humorous streak, and a generous and giving nature. I remembered meeting him thinking he was cruel and self-absorbed. How wrong I was to judge him so quickly and harshly. Jones was a lot of things, but selfish and cold were not among them.

I laughed, thinking how I once believed he had *small dick syndrome*. Nothing could be further from the truth. Jones's face tightened when I laughed, his dark expression ominous. He was all business and I was killing his energy.

"Lay down on the bed and remove your pants." I laid my body out over the fluffy white duvet and lifted my hips. "Slowly," he barked when I shimmied them down too quickly. "Take your time, Adam. I'm enjoying the show."

With my pants off and my legs bare, I scissored them impatiently as I toyed with the waistband of my briefs.

"Feeling inspired? Go on, then. Make it look good for me."

He lingered over the buttons of his shirt, teasing me as he slowly undid each one, revealing glimpses of the dark hair that lightly furred his broad chest.

Fuck, he was spinning my head in circles. Nothing got me hotter than when he took command of my pleasure. I worked the elastic over one hip as I spread my thighs wide. Then the other hip. My hard cock bounced free, slapping against my belly with a pop. My balls were smooth and tight as I exposed them to the cool air.

"Tease yourself, Adam. I want to see you so needy that your pretty cock drips for me."

His words alone were enough to get it started. As I fingered my cock, Jones slowly removed each article of clothing from his hard body. No other man had ever affected me the way he did. I was desperate for him, and he hadn't even touched me yet. Only Jones could do that to me. I traced my fingertips over my sac, down my taint, to flirt with my hole.

"Turn over, Adam. Give me a better view."

He palmed his hard cock, teasing himself with long, slow strokes. My eyes widened as I tracked his movements, imagining it was my hand that gripped his hard length.

Fuck, he was going to tear my ass up tonight. I rolled onto my stomach and braced my weight on my chest as I popped my ass in the air, thighs spread wide. I dragged my fingers through my crease, ghosting over my hole.

"It's too dry," I complained.

Jones leaned forward and spit on my exposed hole. It was filthy and hot and made me desperate to be fucked. I worked his thick saliva into my hole, using two fingers to open myself up. Knowing he watched was almost enough to make me beg for his cock.

"Is two enough to take me? Better add a third, I'm really hard."

He chuckled with satisfaction when I whimpered. Heeding his implied threat that he intended to split me open roughly, I worked a third finger into my channel and fucked my fingers until I felt loose and primed.

"Please, sir?" He loved it when I begged. If I was able to look, I bet I'd see his crown was dark and wet, ready to enter me.

Cold liquid, most likely lube, drizzled down my crease. Jones trailed the tip of his finger around my hole, circling my fingers, before pushing inside. He slicked my hole well so I could easily accept his girth. The bundle of fingers stuffed inside me made my skin burn from the wide stretch. His weight dipped the mattress behind me, the heat of his body warm as he climbed between my thighs and rubbed his swollen cockhead through my slippery crack. Jones dragged the head of his dick down the length of my hard cock, back-and-forth from root to tip, tracing the thick vein, teasing until I wanted to scream. Then I felt his blunt head push against my tight pucker as he shoved force-fully inside.

"Ahh!" I cried out, the stretch and burn was almost too much.

"You can take it, sweetheart. Just a little more before I'm all the way home."

He covered my body with his, the weight of him holding me prisoner beneath him, his warm breath heavy in my ear. Jones sank his teeth into the thick skin on the back of my neck as he buried himself deep inside my body.

Damn, his words set me on fire! I would gladly take a bite of pain for him, to have him buried inside me, consuming me with his need. I pushed back against him and locked my feet around his ankles, using the leverage to fuck myself on his dick.

"That's it, baby. Show me what you want. Is that how you like it?"

His thrusts matched mine, deep, hard, driving strokes that left me crying out in ecstasy each time his body moved against mine. There was no slap of skin against skin. There was no space between our bodies. Jones's flesh was molded to mine, he couldn't be any deeper, closer, unless he was inside of me. With his next powerful thrust, I was convinced that was his goal. His hands drew mine out above my head, his fingers laced through mine as he worked my body to the point of exhaustion. I lay in a boneless, sweaty, sated heap as he continued to pound my ass.

"Work my cock, Adam."

I found a reserve of energy and took over while he fidgeted with my hand. Cool metal kissed the skin of my ring finger, and I paused to look up at my hand in his. His black titanium ring with the row of embedded diamonds was transferred to my hand now. Jones gripped my fingers, curling them in his strong fist.

"That's my ring, baby. It's yours now. I'm yours, as well. Just as you're mine. Look at it while I fuck my load into your tight ass. When I'm finished, and I've satisfied you, you can give me your answer."

I panted rapidly as he ground my weeping cock into the mattress with each stroke. "Your ass was made for my cock, just as you were made for me," he grunted savagely.

Jones sucked dark bruises into my neck, across my shoulders, marking every inch of my body as his as he bred me relentlessly. I had one thought swirl through my mind, screaming loud and clear over the pounding of my heart.

Yes! Fuck, yes!

But I refused to give in so easily. Jones deserved to work for it. He loved the challenge. I couldn't disappoint him.

"I'm about to fill your hole, so if you want to come, better do it now."

He sheathed himself deep inside my tight heat as his dick pulsed thick ropes of cum inside my ass. It killed me not to follow, but it would feel even sweeter to wait it out.

Jones collapsed on my back, sweating and panting. "Fuck." His fingers trailed down my spine, over the swell of my ass, to where our bodies joined. "I might leave it in another minute until you answer me."

My lips curved into a sexy challenging smirk. "I don't recall you asking me a question?"

His pale blue eyes narrowed. "Turn over."

Carefully, he withdrew from my well-used body, and I rolled beneath his heavy weight. On my back, I looked into his flushed, rugged face.

"Adam Wells, will you be mine? Will you spend the rest of your life as my husband?"

I didn't know how much I needed to hear the words until he spoke them. But I still wouldn't give him the satisfaction of an answer.

"I'm sorry, I can't hear you clearly without your lips stretched around my cock."

His wicked smile mirrored mine as he slid down the length of my damp body, eyes on mine as his tongue licked a warm path down to my still-hard cock. He slipped it between his lips and hummed around my girth, sending shivers down my shaft, straight to my balls. Damn, I was teetering on the edge, just waiting to hear the words again before I shot down his throat. My hands tangled in his dark hair, gripping the silky strands between my fingers as I held his head in place.

"Still can't hear you, sir."

He squeezed my sac as he took me to the back of his throat and my eyes crossed. His words sounded garbled spoken around my thick shaft, but I made them out with crystal clarity.

"Marry me, Adam."

I pushed his head down to choke on my dick as I

flooded his mouth, loving his watery eyes and the sound of his gag. He swallowed most of it, licked his lips, and crawled up my body to feed me the last few precious drops. Jones slotted his mouth over mine, coaxing my lips apart, his silky tongue gliding along mine. He stroked my mouth to ecstasy as I fed from the bitter sweetness of his.

When I broke the heated kiss to gasp for breath, my eyes landed on the framed picture on his nightstand. We were dressed in our gay reindeer sweaters, me feeding him a piece of my homemade biscotti. His smile was warm and happy, a complete turnaround from his normal stoic expression.

I did that.

His eyes were focused on me, and he was smiling—at me. *Because of me.* It was hard for me to imagine a man as powerful and independent as Jones could fall for a man like me, make me feel like he needed me. But as I stared at the proof, I knew without a doubt it was true. Jones wouldn't rest until I said yes because he always got what he wanted.

And he wanted me.

Jones mistook my silence as a negative. He gripped my face, bringing my attention back to him. "I'm not asking, I'm begging, Adam."

A small smile pulled at the corners of my mouth. "I thought you once said you don't ask and you never beg."

Jones nipped my lips. "You're worth breaking every one of my rules." He tugged my hand with the ring up to his lips and sucked my finger into his warm wet mouth.

"We can have a long engagement. I just want to know that you're mine."

"I am yours. I don't need a ring to prove it to you, but I'll gladly wear it anyway."

His lips caressed the black metal lovingly. "Happy New Year's Eve, Adam."

EPILOGUE

Jones

The cool wind bit at my cheeks and whipped my hair into disarray. Not that it mattered. With the sun shining, the seagulls crying overhead, and the tang of salty air in my nose, I felt euphoric as I stood on the deck of my boat, next to the man who would become my husband in a matter of minutes.

Adam never looked sexier as he beamed at me, his hand tucked into mine. The dove gray fitted pants I chose for him showcased his beautiful ass to perfection. My fingers itched to grope him, but it would have to wait until after our reception. The gray and ivory corset vest made his chiseled chest appear even broader. His warm, golden skin glowed against the white button-down shirt. With his sleeves rolled up, highlighting his thick, veiny forearms, Adam looked mouthwatering.

And with my ring on his finger, he looked like *mine*.

Adam chose a similar band for me, but with sapphires instead of diamonds, to remind me of his eyes. Like I needed a reminder—everything about him was front and center in my mind every time I closed my eyes. Adam was everything I'd dreamed of having but denied myself for years. I had finally come into my own, and I could count my lucky stars that he chose to stand by my side and take my name.

My coworkers, some of my clients, and all of Adam's friends, including his parents, stood on the long wooden dock. The boat was anchored in its slip at the marina, and with our slip being the last in line, we had an uninhibited view of the bay. A magistrate, dressed in black, stood before us, clutching a tiny book in his hands. This was not a religious ceremony, the book held quotes and snippets of poems Adam had wanted.

And what Adam wanted, Adam got. Nothing brought me more pleasure than catering to his wishes. There was no greater satisfaction than making him feel that he was worth being spoiled.

I turned to Adam—my partner, my future—and prepared to say the words that would make him my husband.

The magistrate spoke loud enough for the assembled guests to hear. "Jones, place your ring on Adam's finger and recite your vows."

It pained me to remove his ring last night for the ceremony today, but pomp and circumstance won out. Adam offered me his hand, which I held securely in my left hand as I used my right to slide the cool black titanium onto his fourth finger.

"Adam Wells, I take you as my husband, to cherish, honor, and protect, all the days of my life. I vow to always strive to put your needs above my own, and to never forget how lucky I am that you chose to spend your life with me."

It made me smile fondly to see his beautiful sapphire eyes mist. Adam had the purest, softest heart, and I valued it above everything. It wasn't often that I met a man with such perfect packaging who wasn't selfish, greedy, and shallow. Adam was none of those things. He was a unicorn, a rare species of man who had an abundance of desirable qualities—he was the total package.

Jesus fuck, I hit the jackpot.

～

Adam

I COULDN'T HAVE ASKED for more perfect weather. Cold and windy, but absolutely beautiful. The view from the deck of his boat overlooking the bay looked as if it were painted by the hand of God. Everyone I loved and cared for was here to witness my wedding to a man who, despite being my complete opposite in every way, was perfectly matched with me.

Our relationship thus far had been a dizzying whirlwind of steamy nights, adventurous days, long walks and long talks, and a wicked learning curve a mile wide.

Jones could be...difficult...at times, to say the least, and other times, completely amenable. He was a man of many moods, but he was always in the mood for love.

Sharing my life with him would never be boring.

The magistrate smiled at me. "Adam, place your ring on Jones's finger and recite your vows."

My hand was already warmly ensconced in his sure grip. I loosened his hold and reached in my pocket for the ring, sliding it into place as I stared into his eyes.

"Jones Marin, I take you as my husband, to cherish, honor, and protect, all the days of my life. I vow to always strive to be patient with you, loyal, honest, and to never forget how grateful I am to have found you."

I raised his hand to my lips and pressed a kiss to the sapphire-studded ring. Jones's eyes flared with heat, making me wish everyone suddenly melted away and we were all alone. Lowering our joined hands, I refocused on the officiant and smiled.

He looked fondly at our joined hands, then his eyes swept over our grinning, expectant faces. "With the power vested in me by the state of South Carolina, I pronounce you married!"

Jones took me in his strong arms and dipped me backwards. His soft lips devoured my mouth, stroking my tongue indecently in front of our guests as they cheered. It was the best kiss.

As soon as Jones released his hold on me, I was flooded with congratulations, hugs, and kisses from my mother, the ladies of the EWC, and my friends.

Murphy punched my arm playfully. "You lucky

fucker! You snagged yourself a sexy sugar daddy. Way to go, Adam."

I would have flushed with embarrassment if the remark hadn't been expected and typical for Murphy Maguire.

My usually stoic husband completely surprised me when he laughed. "He sure did. And I snagged a hot young piece of ass. I guess an old dog can still learn new tricks."

The reception on board the boat was short and sweet. The catered hor d'oeuvres tasted delicious, champagne flowed, and the dessert table was laden with a tiered citrus and cream cheese frosted cake and, of course, my homemade chocolate dipped biscotti.

When it was time to cut the cake, Jones cut a small slice, took it between his fingers, and fed it to me, sliding the tips of his fingers between my lips. Then, he chased the cake with his mouth, kissing me hungrily with my mouth full of dessert, as he ate a bite of cake from the inside of my mouth. It was dirty and decadent and signaled the end of the party.

Jones and I stayed aboard after saying goodbye to our guests. We were headed to the Turks and Caicos Islands for our honeymoon—a week alone together under the sun.

I felt the heat of his body warm my back as he approached me from behind. Perched at the rail, overlooking the bay, I envisioned my future married to the complex, amazing man who was now my husband.

Damn! I hit the jackpot.

His warm breath ghosted over my ear. "I love you with all my heart, Adam Marin."

Jones turned his mouth to meet mine, sliding his silky tongue between my lips. He tasted of sugar from the cake, and I devoured his sweet kiss.

"I'm head over heels in love with you, too."

"I promised you we would someday take this boat on a real vacation, and I delivered."

"You also promised me another round in the salon upstairs. Do you plan to consummate this marriage?" I teased him with the press of my ass against his groin.

Jones groaned in my ear. "I'm tempted to fuck you over this railing, Mr. Marin. But first, we have something important to discuss."

I turned to face him. Jones slid his arms around my waist, pulling me in close to his warm, hard body. "Is everything okay?"

Heat sparked in Jones's pale blue eyes. "You left something important out of your vows. You forgot to promise to obey me." He pressed a kiss to my chin.

I untangled my body from his hold and headed for the stairs that led to the glass-enclosed sundeck. When I reached the railing, I glanced back, a coy smile tugged at my lips.

"It's open for discussion. If you'll follow me, we can negotiate our terms."

The End

Want more of the male escorts of Lucky Match?

Download the first book in the series, **Lucky Match**, and get caught up with all the boys from the **Hearts For Hire** series today!

～

CHECK out Carson and Shannon and the sexy staff of *Limericks Lounge* in the **Love And Libations series**, available now on Amazon and Kindle Unlimited.

～

Join my Facebook Reader group, **Raquel Riley's Romantics**, to stay up to date on everything happening in Cooper's Cove!

VISIT my website for signed books, digital downloads, merchandise, and much more! **www.raquelriley.com**

DEAR READER

Thank you so much for reading **Hired For The Holidays**, the fifth and final book in the Hearts For Hire series.

If you enjoyed Jones and Adam's romance, **please leave a review** to tell other readers how much you loved them. Telling your friends and spreading the word on social media helps people find their new favorite book.

With love,
Raquel Riley

ALSO BY RAQUEL RILEY

Want to catch up with the Hearts For Hire series? Start from the beginning with Lucky Match and work your way through all of the escorts' happily ever afters!

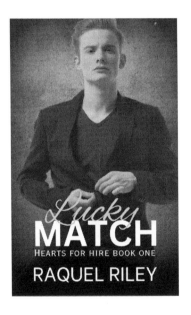

After one date, I realized that would never be enough...

Lucky Maguire

I started Lucky Match, a dating service, as an enjoyable way to earn some extra cash. That's how I ended up on a date with my super hot Economics Professor.

Here's my three step plan to seduce my teacher:

Convince Hayes to fake date me.

Inform him that we were never fake dating; it was always real.

Make him fall in love with me.

How many dates will it take for Hayes to realize I'm his lucky match?

Hayes Brantley

After my divorce, I decided it's time for a change. After missing being with a man for the past twelve years of my loveless marriage, I'm finally free to make up for lost time.

I called Lucky Match to hookup with someone who looks like the sexy student I can't stop fantasizing about. I had no idea I'd end up with the real deal.

Is a second chance at love worth risking my career and another broken heart?

The Hearts For Hire
Series follows five
college roommates
as they start a male
escort service,
Lucky Match.

Each book tells the
story of how each
man finds love on
the job.

MATCH
HEARTS FOR HIRE BOOK ONE
RAQUEL RILEY

FOR YOU
HEARTS FOR HIRE BOOK TWO
RAQUEL RILEY

TOGETHER
HEARTS FOR HIRE BOOK THREE
RAQUEL RILEY

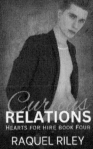

RELATIONS
HEARTS FOR HIRE BOOK FOUR
RAQUEL RILEY

HIRED FOR THE
HEARTS FOR HIRE BOOK FIVE
RAQUEL RILEY

LOVE AND LIBATIONS

The *Love and Libations* series kicks off with a sweet second chances prequel, **Mimosas and Mixers.**

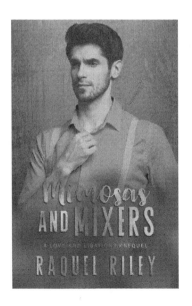

Are you ever too old to fall in love? What are the odds you'll end up with the first boy you ever crushed on?

Nate

Running into Charlie at our high school reunion was kismet. I can't imagine myself with anyone else. Is it too late for a second chance at love?

Charlie

Nate is everything I dreamt of finding in a partner. Except, he's my son's therapist. Will their professional relationship come between our personal one? Or does fate have other plans for us?

Mimosas and Mixers is the prequel to the *Love and Libations* series. This sweet heat gay romance novella includes cameos from the Hearts For Hire Series and features tropes such as second chances, a mature couple, childhood friends, and found family.

Check out the entire completed series, available now on Amazon and Kindle Unlimited!

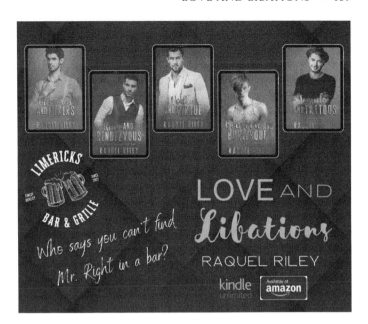

About the Author

Raquel Riley is a native of South Florida but now calls North Carolina home. She is an avid reader and loves to travel. Most often, she writes gay romance stories with an HEA but characters of all types can be found in her books. She weaves pieces of herself, her family, and her travels into every story she writes.

For a complete list of Raquel Riley's releases, please visit her website at **www.raquelriley.com**. You can also follow her on the social media platforms listed below. You can also find all of Raquel's important links in one convenient place at **https://linktr.ee/raquelriley**

ACKNOWLEDGMENTS

Finn Dixon, without your help and considerable talent, this book would have been forever a first draft. I'll never find the right words to tell you how much I appreciate you.

Odessa Hywell, thank you for always answering when I call with endless questions, or just to spitball. You keep me sane.

Tracy Ann, your feedback is so appreciated! Thank you for your continued praise and support of my stories, and for keeping me organized and on task.

Also, thank you to my **ARC/street team** for your insightful input and reviews and outstanding promotion.

A huge thank you to the **86'ers!** You crazy bunch are guaranteed to make me laugh at least fourteen times a day.

I can't forget the **Secret Circle!** You bunch keep me accountable and sane and cheer for every one of my accomplishments, both big and small.

Last, but never least, thanks to my family for being so understanding while I ignore you so I can write.

I hope you continue the fun by checking out **Mimosas And Mixers**!

Made in the USA
Columbia, SC
22 December 2024